"The fact is, someone in this building is pregnant with my baby. And I need your help to find her."

"Pregnant?" Maggie whispered, stunned. Had she heard Kane right? "How? I mean, wouldn't you know who she is?"

Kane shook his head. "Artificial insemination," he explained curtly. "It was a big mix-up. That was why I wanted you to get in touch with the fertility clinic I asked you to call. It happened there."

"Oh." A funny little tune was playing in her head. "No, no, no," seemed to be the words.

"Maggie, I've tried to do this on my own, but I've struck out every time. I really need your help. You know a lot of the women here. I'm sure you could get a line on who she might be. She should be about five months pregnant...."

She shook her head. This couldn't be happening. "No, no, no," she said softly.

"Maggie," he said, surprise in his voice. He reached for her. "What's wrong?"

"I'm five months pregnant."

Dear Reader,

Brr… February's below-freezing temperatures call for a mug of hot chocolate, a fuzzy afghan and a heartwarming book from Silhouette Romance. Our books will heat you to the tips of your toes with the sizzling sexual tension that courses between our stubborn heroes and the determined heroines who ultimately melt their hardened hearts.

In Judy Christenberry's *Least Likely To Wed,* her sinfully sexy cowboy hero has his plans for lifelong bachelorhood foiled by the searing kisses of a spirited single mom. While in Sue Swift's *The Ranger & the Rescue,* an amnesiac cowboy stakes a claim on the heart of a flame-haired heroine—but will the fires of passion still burn when he regains his memory?

Tensions reach the boiling point in Raye Morgan's *She's Having My Baby!*—the final installment of the miniseries HAVING THE BOSS'S BABY—when our heroine discovers just who fathered her baby-to-be…. And tempers flare in Rebecca Russell's *Right Where He Belongs,* in which our handsome hero must choose between his cold plan for revenge and a woman's warm and tender love.

Then simmer down with the incredibly romantic heroes in Teresa Southwick's *What If We Fall In Love?* and Colleen Faulkner's *A Shocking Request.* You'll laugh, you'll cry, you'll fall in love all over again with these deeply touching stories about widowers who get a second chance at love.

So this February, come in from the cold and warm your heart and spirit with one of these temperature-raising books from Silhouette Romance. Don't forget the marshmallows!

Happy reading!

Mary-Theresa Hussey

Mary-Theresa Hussey
Senior Editor

Please address questions and book requests to:
Silhouette Reader Service
U.S.: 3010 Walden Ave., P.O. Box 1325, Buffalo, NY 14269
Canadian: P.O. Box 609, Fort Erie, Ont. L2A 5X3

Raye Morgan

SHE'S HAVING MY BABY!

SILHOUETTE *Romance*®

Published by Silhouette Books

America's Publisher of Contemporary Romance

Special thanks and acknowledgment are given to Raye Morgan for her contribution to the HAVING THE BOSS'S BABY series.

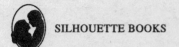

SILHOUETTE BOOKS

ISBN 0-373-19571-0

SHE'S HAVING MY BABY!

Copyright © 2002 by Harlequin Books S.A.

This edition published by arrangement with Harlequin Books S.A.

® and TM are trademarks of Harlequin Books S.A., used under license. Trademarks indicated with ® are registered in the United States Patent and Trademark Office, the Canadian Trade Marks Office and in other countries.

Visit Silhouette at www.eHarlequin.com

Printed in U.S.A.

Books by Raye Morgan

RAYE MORGAN

has spent almost two decades, while writing over fifty novels, searching for the answer to that elusive question: Just what is that special magic that happens when a man and a woman fall in love? Every time she thinks she has the answer, a new wrinkle pops up, necessitating another book! Meanwhile, after living in Holland, Guam, Japan and Washington, D.C., she currently makes her home in Southern California with her husband and two of her four boys.

Note to self: Who's having my baby?

Trudy—hopeless romantic, office gossip, can't keep a secret. *If it's not her, she might know who it is!*

~~Lauren Connor~~—dates a lot, trying out new looks to impress her boss, was out sick with stomach *flu*. *Hmm...*

~~Sharon Davies~~—recently trapped in an elevator with a major client, blushes whenever he's around, looking a little green lately. *Could she be carrying my baby?*

Leila—makes eyes at me. *Is it more than a crush?*

Maggie Steward—my personal assistant, wants children, clock is ticking. *She would never go to a sperm bank!*

~~Julia Parker~~—worries that her endometriosis could make her infertile. No man in her life. *Definite sperm bank material!*

~~Jennifer Martin~~—eight months pregnant. Is it her late fiancé's baby? *Is it mine?*

WHEN THE LIGHTS WENT OUT... October 2001
A PREGNANT PROPOSAL November 2001
THE MAKEOVER TAKEOVER December 2001
LAST CHANCE FOR BABY January 2002
SHE'S HAVING MY BABY! February 2002

KANE HALEY, INC.
Chicago, IL

Chapter One

Kane Haley was staring at her with that weird look again. Maggie Steward bit her lip and leaned forward toward her computer monitor so that her crisp navy blue linen jacket would fall out and hide her stomach. Her heart was thumping. Had her boss guessed she was pregnant?

She went back to typing up the letter he'd asked her to write and wished he would close the door to his wood-paneled office so she couldn't see him sitting in there, staring out at her. And even more important, so *he* couldn't see *her*.

She should have told him by now. She'd meant to. But she just hadn't found the right words. Once he knew she was going to have a baby, she had a feeling things would change drastically—not only professionally, but personally.

Nervously, she pushed a stray strand of golden-blond hair back into the twist at the nape of her neck and tried to concentrate on what she was doing, but thoughts and regrets were straying as well. Once he found out, she had no idea what he might say or do. What if he decided he needed someone he could depend on over the next few months? What if he asked her to transfer to another department so he could begin training someone new?

She valued her job as his administrative assistant, but more than that, she really needed it. The money was much better than for any other position she could qualify for in the company. And finances were turning out to be much tighter than she'd expected. She had no one to depend on but herself. Having a baby cost so much money!

The letter was finished and sliding slowly out of the printer. Ordinarily, she would go right in and have him sign it, but she was hesitating, worrying about what he might be thinking. Was he framing the question right now? Was he wondering why she hadn't told him?

Maggie! Get a grip!

She scolded herself and rose from her ergonomically correct chair, being very careful not to move in any way that might emphasize her pregnancy, grabbed the letter and marched right into his office.

"Mr. Haley, if you'll sign this, I'll get it out right away."

"Hmm?" He gazed at her blankly.

As always when her eyes met his, there was a little frisson of excitement that scattered along her nerve endings. Just one of the hazards of working for a man who looked like a cross between a young U.S. senator and a cowboy—smoothly handsome grace leavened by a core toughness that defined masculinity at its best, as far as she was concerned.

"Oh," he said as he realized what she was there for. Picking up a pen, he held out his other hand for the page. "Sure."

She waited apprehensively for his gaze to make a quick trip down toward her slightly protruding stomach, for his eyes to narrow and his brows to furl, but it didn't happen. He signed the paper, tossed the pen down and stared into space again, ignoring her completely, his mind obviously captivated by some puzzle that wouldn't let him be.

She frowned, turning her head to see what he was looking at, then turned back again, muffling a sigh of relief. Thank goodness. He hadn't been staring at her at all. He was staring into space, and the space he was staring into just happened to be in her direction. He hadn't noticed a thing. Her heart lightened.

Still, something about all this staring did bother her. She cleared her throat, and when that didn't conjure up a response, she added crisply, "Do you have those notes on the new estimates ready for me to incorporate into the contract for the Bellingham people?"

"Contract?" His dark eyes flashed her way, and

then he seemed to shake himself back to the present. "Oh, the notes for the contract. Don't worry, I'll take care of them." He glanced at the cluttered surface of his desk and made a vague gesture. "They're around here somewhere."

"It's got to be in the mail by five," she reminded him.

He gave her a long-suffering look. "I know that. And I'll have them ready for you."

She raised an eyebrow. "Sure you will," she said, lightly mocking him in a way that she'd become accustomed to and he usually enjoyed. "By four fifty-seven, no doubt."

But he'd already forgotten she was standing alongside his desk. His dark-eyed gaze had glazed over and taken on a faraway look again.

She watched him, frowning, her gaze sliding from his handsome face to his wide shoulders to his strong but idle hands. This was not good, and it wasn't like him. His mind wasn't on his work. She'd been noticing that more and more often lately. What was going on?

Walking back toward her desk, she carefully closed the door to his office, then went over possibilities of disaster as she slid into her seat. What if he was thinking about changing his life in some way? What if he was bored and wanted to start a new business in some other place? What if he was about to quit his position and sail around the world on a catamaran? He'd talked about doing that once—gone on and on about the romance of the high seas.

"Just man against the ocean," he'd told her, striking a pose, as though he had the mast at his back and a headwind before him. "What could be more thrilling?"

A steady paycheck, that was what. She didn't want him to go anywhere. Not only would she lose her job, she would lose...him. Her cheeks reddened even though there was no one there to see them. She had to stop thinking about him like that.

Of course, there was no use pretending she hadn't had a low-level crush on him from the beginning. What red-blooded woman wouldn't find a man like Kane Haley attractive? But she'd never for a moment held out any hope that he might look at her in a romantic way. She was a person of common sense, and her instincts told her she wasn't the sort of woman a man like Kane fell for.

And that was okay. She had her own life to live— a life that had become a little more lonely since her husband Tom had died in a car accident coming home from a deer-hunting trip two years ago. Glancing down at her left hand, she was startled to realize it had been almost six months since she'd taken off her wedding and engagement rings. It still surprised her whenever she noticed they weren't there. She'd been a new widow when she'd been promoted to cover for Kane's assistant who'd been out on maternity leave, and she'd thrown her heart into her work. When the woman had decided to stay home with her baby, Maggie had already fit in so well, Kane had asked her to stay on permanently. It was a dream of a job and he was a dream of a boss. She adored him.

What he thought of her was a little more ambiguous. Did he think about her at all? Sadly, evidence suggested he didn't pay much attention to her in any way except as an efficient manager of his time and business affairs.

Even more annoying, sometimes she actually had a feeling that Kane Haley thought she was still married. He'd said something in passing about her husband a couple of times, and she'd let it go, thinking it really didn't matter. After all, their relationship was totally work-related. But a little part of her had wondered if she should make it clear to him that she was free, just in case....

But that was going nowhere. He was a terrific boss. Their relationship was very special to her. She wouldn't do anything to ruin it if she could help it. She only hoped he wasn't planning anything that would do exactly that.

Of course, her decision to go ahead and have a baby might be enough to put a damper on things. It had all seemed so easy back when she'd begun. Lately, she'd had second thoughts. Not about the baby—but about her timing. Things just weren't falling into place the way she'd hoped.

With a sigh, she went back to work at her computer, resolving to think of a way to tell him she was pregnant.

"Gotta do it today," she promised the empty air. "No more excuses."

Kane watched Maggie walk away and close the door behind her and he groaned with envy. There went a woman without a worry in the world. She was the most efficient assistant he'd ever had, always on top of every situation, always ready with a calm smile and a quick retort when he needed snapping into shape. He couldn't remember how he'd managed before she'd appeared like Mary Poppins to organize his life. He really didn't know what he'd do without her. Sometimes he thought she knew more about what made his company run than he did. She was terrific. Her husband was a lucky man. He couldn't help but wonder if she ran as tight a ship at home as she ran here. Did she keep her husband in line, too?

Odd that in almost two years of working together, he'd never met her husband. But that seemed to fit with the coolly detached way she handled things between the two of them. She never got personal, and neither did he. She was all business and she ran this place, to all intents and purposes.

And that was a good thing, too, especially right now, because his work was going to hell lately, and he knew it. He had his mind on only one thing and it was driving him nuts. If he didn't find out soon just who in this company was carrying his baby, he was going to go crazy.

Closing his eyes, he swore softly. *Crazy.* That was a good word for this situation. It had started out in a relatively sane and sober way. When his good friend, Bill Jeffers, had had a cancer scare and had come to him about it, he'd been ready to do anything he could to help out. He'd taken Bill to see his cousin, a world-class oncologist, and then had gone with him to the various testing labs, including the clinic where Bill was encouraged to deposit sperm to be used in case his radiation treatments destroyed his chances of ever having children. Kane himself had been surprised when the technician suggested he deposit some as well, to put Bill, who was quite nervous, at ease. Of course, he'd been glad to do anything to help his friend at this tense time.

The radiation treatments were, thank God, successful, and Bill was fine today. Just a few months ago, Bill had called to let him know he and his new wife Tracy were going to have a baby.

"You didn't have to make use of that little deposit you made at the clinic that day, did you?" Kane had asked him, jokingly.

Bill had assured him it hadn't been necessary, but once Kane had hung up, he'd begun thinking about his own deposit. He hadn't ever done anything about it. It really wasn't one of those things you should leave hanging around. The next morning, he'd called the clinic to tell them to have it destroyed. And that was when this nightmare had begun.

When he'd found out that his sample had been mistakenly used just weeks before—and by someone who worked in his company—he'd been stunned. The clinic had adamantly refused to tell him the name of the woman, even though he'd threatened legal action. And he'd been trying ever since to figure out which of the many women who worked at Kane Haley, Inc., was walking around incubating his baby!

"Let it go," his brother Mark had said just that morning when they were playing their usual Friday racquetball game at their health club. "Forget about it. It's out of your hands. You really aren't involved in any meaningful way. Get over it!"

"I can't," he replied glumly, giving the ball a vicious slash. "You don't understand."

Mark, with his bouncy redheaded wife and his two bright kids in his beautiful house in one of the nicest suburban villages in the Chicago area, really *didn't* understand. How could he? His life had been smooth sailing from day one. Kane didn't resent his happiness, but he was sharply aware of the differences in their experiences, despite having grown up more or less in the same family. Mark believed in happy marriages, for one thing. He had one. Kane knew from his own past—including a very miserable marriage—that they were few and far between.

"There's just no way of finding this woman," Mark went on. "And even if you found her, what could you do about it?'' He dodged a ball that came ricocheting off the wall at him, batting it down to where he could handle it and toss it back to his brother. "Give it up."

"I've got to find her." Kane served an ace and felt a glow of triumph as Mark flailed at it and missed. "I can't rest until I do."

Mark winced, shaking his head as he looked back at his brother. "Why?" he asked simply.

In answer, Kane hit the ball just right again and practically laid Mark out against the wall. The sound the hard ball made against the wood echoed through the little enclosed court and he grinned and flexed his biceps. Served Mark right. It was high time he learned to treat his older brother with a little respect.

Unfortunately, respect didn't seem to last the way it once had, and in minutes, Mark was in charge of the service, putting across his own winning aces. Kane's attention evaporated along with his game. His mind was back on his problem, and his brother could tell.

Hitting another hard one, Mark asked again, insisting, "Why?"

"Because," Kane said in exasperation, letting the ball go by and not even reacting to it. "Just because. I can't help it." He knew his voice was sounding choked, but he had to try to make his brother understand. "I've got to find my baby. Mark, it's like a fire smoldering inside of me. The need to find him haunts me all the time."

Mark stopped and turned toward him, frowning. He hesitated, then went ahead and spoke softly. "Kane, it isn't your baby. You gave it away."

Anger flared in his heart, but he managed to keep his voice low and steady as he dropped down to sit on the lowest step of the stairway out of the court. "That wasn't my doing." He was forcing himself to breathe evenly, to keep this under control.

"Maybe not, but it was done." Mark slumped down beside him. "Hell, Kane, go out and find some woman and marry her and make your own baby. Forget about the sperm thing. It's over."

He looked at his brother and laughed softly. "Come on, man, do you think the old lord of the manor cared about the kids he fathered when he went out rolling in the haystack with the milkmaids? This is like a modern-day version. After all, you're president of the company. Your employees are like the old-fashioned tenants on the land." He frowned comically. "Same deal, except with these twenty-first-century methods, I think you're getting rooked out of the fun part."

Kane avoided his gaze, shaking his head. "This isn't funny, Mark. I'm quite serious about it. I'm going to find my baby."

Mark put a hand on his arm. "And do what once you do? Ruin things for some nice young couple who managed to get pregnant with your help? Don't you think they would be much happier not knowing you're involved?" He hesitated and his voice softened with sympathy. "Come on, Kane. Whoever she is isn't going to want you in her life. Face facts. You'd be nothing but an intrusion."

Kane looked Mark in the eye. "You may be right, but I have to know." He tried to smile at his brother, but his emotions were running too close to the surface to risk it. "Anyway, I could be a help to them. I could be like an uncle. I could come at Christmas with gifts for everyone. I could make sure he had a college education...."

Mark groaned and rose, heading for the showers. "You're hopeless," he tossed back over his shoulder. "I give up."

But Kane wouldn't give up. He couldn't give up. His baby was out there somewhere. It was just a matter of time before he would know where.

He had a thing about kids and their fathers, a special need that had a lot of history attached to it. Back in his office, pacing the beige carpet until a path was being worn in it, he knew one thing for sure. Somehow, he was going to find out where his child was.

But what could he do next? He'd already harassed four women who worked at Kane Haley, Inc., thinking each might be the one because of one thing or another. False leads each time, but he'd tried, damn it. And now, as far as he knew, there weren't any pregnant women left.

Running a hand through his thick hair, he frowned. He was going to have to go back to the clinic. He just couldn't see any other way. He was going to have to threaten legal action again, and force them to tell him who she was.

Either that, or sign himself up for full-time therapy.

Flopping down in his office chair, he reached forward and clicked on the interoffice communicator. "Maggie," he said crisply.

"Yes, sir?"

"Look up the number of the Lakeside Reproductive Clinic..."

The gasp on the other end of the line interrupted him.

"Are you okay?"

"Yes." She sounded breathless, but her voice was strong. "Yes. Did you say the Lakeside...?"

"Lakeside Reproductive Clinic. That's the one. I want you to put in a call to the chief of operations for me, will you? Put him right through when you get him. Thanks."

Kane leaned back in his chair, drumming his fingers on the desk pad and marshaling his arguments. It was time to get tough.

Chapter Two

Maggie looked down at her hands. They were still shaking. When Mr. Haley had told her to call the Lakeside Reproductive Clinic, she'd nearly had a heart attack. That was the very clinic where she'd undergone artificial insemination just five months ago. What on earth did he want to talk to them about?

Whatever it was would have to wait until Monday. She'd made the call, but the clinic was closed on Fridays. He would have to call back next week. When she'd told him, he'd growled, but he hadn't given as much as a clue as to what business he had with them.

Taking a deep breath, she tried to settle herself. All right. This was it. She had to find the words to tell her boss that she was pregnant, and she had to do it right away. She couldn't go on like this.

A sound from behind made her jump, but it was only the company mail delivery.

"Hi, CeCe," she said to the short, dark-haired woman counting out envelopes to leave in her box. "So what's new out there in the Kane Haley, Incorporated, world?"

"Well, let's see," CeCe offered, narrowing her dark eyes as she thought things over. "Jolene Brown on the third floor says since we're putting in a day-care center for the babies, we should have one for pets, too."

"Pets!"

"Yup. Seems she's having trouble with a new Yorkie she inherited. It's eating up her house while she's gone, one room at a time. She'd rather have him here where she can keep an eye on him."

"Call a dog psychologist," Maggie suggested with a laugh.

CeCe nodded. "I'll pass on your advice," she promised, turning to go. "Meanwhile, got any hot rumors you want me to spread?"

"Rumors?" Maggie's smile faltered. "No, of course not. Why do you ask?"

CeCe looked at her curiously. "No reason," she said slowly, narrowing her eyes. "No reason at all."

And Maggie cursed her own guilty reaction as the woman left, her mail cart squeaking. "Way to go, Maggie," she scolded herself. "Nothing like planting a seed in fertile ground."

The phone rang and she jumped, grabbing it.

"Hello?" she said breathlessly, expecting bad news, just because it seemed to be that sort of day.

"Maggie?" Her friend Sharon sounded surprised. "Are you okay?"

"Oh." Maggie tried to laugh. "Of course I am. I was just...sort of rushing around here when you called and you startled me."

"Oh." Sharon sounded a bit bewildered, but ready to accept the explanation as offered. "Well, listen. A bunch of us are going out to the Copper Penny for lunch, and I was just wondering...would you like to come along?"

Maggie grimaced. It was awfully nice of Sharon to include her. As the administrative assistant to Kane Haley, she didn't often get treated like "one of the girls." And she loved the Copper Penny. They had the greatest Caesar salads. But she knew she had to decline.

"I'd love to, Sharon, but I'm afraid I've got too much work to do."

The work wasn't the reason. Money was. She couldn't afford to go out to lunch any longer. She had to save every cent for her baby.

"I think I'll just stay in the office and have a sandwich," she told her friend.

"You want me to bring you one back?"

"No. No," she said quickly. "Thanks, though. I brought one from home."

"Okay. We'll miss you."

She chatted with her friend for another moment,

then hung up, smiling as she replaced the receiver, but feeling just a hint of envy. Sharon was pregnant, too, but she wasn't hiding it. And she had a group of good friends to support her, not to mention the baby's father. It must be nice having all that help.

Suddenly Maggie felt very much alone. Placing her hand over her stomach, she thought of her baby. Was she really sure she'd done the right thing? Was she going to be able to make it on her own? And was it fair to her child? She wished she'd waited a while longer before doing this. If only she'd confided in a few people, talked it over, listened to some other experiences before she'd jumped into this. Now she was about to make her boss her only confidant. Nothing was turning out to be the way she'd expected.

Pushing aside doubts, she got very busy during the next half hour or so, and had to run down to Financial to discuss some statistics they'd sent up that morning. When she returned, she assumed her boss had gone out to lunch. She knew Hannah and Kate, the two secretaries in the adjoining office, had gone. The building was quiet. Everyone was either off at a restaurant or down in the cafeteria. Pulling her paper bag out of a bottom drawer, she spread the contents out on her desk and looked at it.

One simple peanut butter sandwich on wheat bread, with just a touch of marmalade, one little box of dried cranberries and an apple. She'd had the same thing for lunch every day for the last month. Staring down at it, she tried to work up some enthusiasm.

"Eating at your desk again?" Kane Haley came out of his office, startling her. He peered at her lunch bag, then at her paltry meal. "Peanut butter sandwiches?"

"They are very nutritious," she replied defensively, unwrapping the plastic and placing the sandwich out on a napkin as she glanced his way.

He was so handsome, his skin tanned even in the depths of winter, his dark hair just unruly enough to look casual. All in all, he was a very sexy guy. Funny how she seemed to be noticing that more and more lately.

He raised one sleek dark eyebrow as he gazed at her skimpy sandwich with a sardonic twist to his mouth. "I'm sure they're full of good things. But not exactly gourmet fare."

"I can't afford gourmet fare at this point." She looked away quickly, feeling flustered and wishing he would go on toward the elevator and leave her alone.

But he seemed in no hurry to leave. Instead of heading for the exit, he casually propped himself on the corner of her desk, one leg swinging, as though he were planning to oversee her lunching activities.

"Why Maggie," he said, his voice warm with teasing humor. "Are you angling for a raise?"

Her eyes widened. "No, sir, I…"

He laughed. "Don't worry. I put in a great evaluation for you just last week. I'm sure there will be something for you when Personnel gets through with their calculations."

"Oh." She wanted to thank him, but she didn't want to sound too desperate. Even if she was exactly that. "I'm...well, thank you very much, Mr. Haley."

"Don't thank me." His smile made her toes curl. "Your work is tops and you know it. I'd rather lose an arm than lose you."

That did it. Guilt choked her. How was she going to tell him? He'd been so great to her and here she was, pretty much betraying him with this pregnancy. No matter how she worked it, she was bound to leave him in the lurch for a few months. There was just no way she could avoid it. Was there? She tried to think, but nothing came to mind. Unless she could work out a way to deliver her baby in the conference room and keep it stashed in the closet and never miss a minute of work. But she had a sneaking suspicion that wouldn't work out. She was going to have to take some time off.

But luckily Mr. Haley was firmly behind the new day-care center that was being set up, right here in the building. She was planning to get her baby into it as soon as possible. But in the meantime, she was going to be leaving him in the lurch. And she felt downright crummy about it.

"Aren't you going out to lunch, Mr. Haley?" she asked pointedly, hoping to jog his memory and speed him out the door.

He sighed, and, for the first time, she noticed that he was looking preoccupied again, despite his sense of humor. "No," he said in answer to her question. "I don't think I'll go out. I can't really eat anything."

She studied him, concerned. He looked tired. Suddenly she wished with all her heart that she knew what was wrong. If she knew what was troubling him, maybe she could help.

"You don't have any children, do you Maggie?"

Her shocked gaze met his and she flushed. How could she answer that one? "N...no. Not...not really." Not yet, anyway. Was that lying? Technically, she didn't think so, but she didn't like it even so.

But he didn't seem to notice her unease. He had a hint of that faraway look again. "I just wonder what it would be like to have a kid," he said softly. Absently, he picked up one half of her peanut butter sandwich and began to munch on it. "Do you ever wonder?" he asked, looking into her eyes as though he thought an answer might be hiding in there somewhere.

Maggie's breath caught in her throat. He was sitting so close and his eyes were so dark.... Suddenly she was very much aware of how the way he was sitting revealed the muscularity of his thighs.

Thighs! What was she thinking? She shouldn't be noticing that. Swallowing hard, she tried to keep some perspective.

"Yes. Yes, of course I wonder," she murmured, but she hardly knew what she was agreeing to.

"There's something almost magical about babies, don't you think?" he was saying.

But she was losing her train of thought. Her attention had been captured by the realization that his eyelashes were incredibly long. Why that made her feel light-headed she couldn't have said. But she stared at them, fascinated, and the room faded around him. He had the most gorgeous eyes she'd ever seen. Weren't eyes supposed to be windows into the heart? Did he have a beautiful soul to match his wonderful eyes?

She was swaying toward him and she knew it, almost as though he were drawing her closer magnetically, and somehow she seemed to be powerless to stop herself. Those deep eyes, the tiny hairs curling at his hairline, the tanned skin—masculinity radiated from him like heat. She came ever closer, experiencing his pull, taking in his air of casual acceptance, his handsome face, his straight nose...the peanut butter on his lower lip.

"Can you pass me a napkin?" he was asking.

She blinked at him as though he'd just gone off like a camera flash in her eyes, staring at him like a deer in headlights.

But he didn't seem to notice. Looking down, he groaned. "My God, I've eaten your whole sandwich."

Her peanut butter sandwich. She shook herself and reality washed over her like a cold ocean wave. Her heart began to thump in her chest. What was wrong with her? She'd almost made a very big fool of herself. Was it her pregnant condition? She was being irrational. Had he noticed?

"Your whole sandwich," he was saying, looking at her as though it were her fault. "Why did you let me do that?"

Taking a deep breath, she steeled herself and fought hard for distance.

"How was I going to stop you?" she said, managing a tart tone, hoping to wipe away any lingering hints of her recent plunge into near-dementia. "You bolted it down like a starved wolf."

"You're right. But it was tiny. And suddenly I *am* hungry." He looked almost embarrassed as he wiped his mouth with her only napkin. Not actually embarrassed, but almost.

"I'm really sorry." His lopsided grin was meant to make up for it. "Listen," he said impulsively. "I know how to fix everything. I'll take you out to lunch."

She gasped. Quick. She had to think of an excuse. "But it's almost one o'clock. I have to be at my desk by one."

He wasn't buying it. "Hey. Who makes the rules around here?"

"I don't know." She frowned, thinking. She did not want to spend any more time with him if she could help it. That silly little trance she'd gone into might have been a harbinger of things to come if she didn't watch out. She couldn't risk it. Besides, she needed time to think up a good way to tell him she was going to be having a baby. It had to be done today. "I guess *you* do."

"Damn right," he said, sliding off her desk. "Come on. Let's go."

"I...I really can't," she said quickly. "I have so much work and..."

"Nonsense. We're going to lunch. And that's an order."

"Mr. Haley..."

"Besides, I owe you. Remember on Secretary's Day I gave you a rain check?"

How could she forget? He'd done that every year since she'd come to work for him. He'd never been keen on doing the lunch thing. Why now? Why with her?

"I'm not a secretary," she tried feebly.

"Administrative assistants should get special days too," he told her cheerfully. "And this is it. I'm finally going to pay up. You're going to get your lunch."

And the next thing she knew, she was stepping into the elevator, heading for lunch with the boss. And looking back longingly at her little office area, seeing it as a haven, a safe harbor. How long before she would get back to that safety?

This was going to be great.

Kane had a plan. A rather good plan, if he did say so himself. He was going to get his superbly skillful assistant working with him to find his baby. He was sure that she would attack the problem with all her legendary efficiency. He didn't know why he hadn't thought of doing this before. It was perfect.

There was only one flaw he could think of—getting her to do it. Instinctively, he knew she would resist. She would think it was a part of his personal life and she had no role there—and, of course, she was right. But he would have to find a way to convince her.

His current scheme was to use this lunch to build a sense of camaraderie between the two of them, get her to feel like a friend, and then to enlist her in the search. It was underhanded, sneaky, and not very nice. He knew that. But desperate times called for desperate measures. He was going to have to put aside all scruples and go for the throat.

As they entered the building that housed his favorite restaurant, he glanced at her sideways and his gaze accidentally cruised down to where her blouse gaped to show a bit of cleavage. She had nice cleavage. It gave him a little jolt of pleasure to see it, and he didn't even feel guilty about it. After all, it meant nothing. She was married. Out of bounds and absolutely safe.

He put a protective hand at the back of her neck as he ushered her into the restaurant itself, and felt another pleasant sensation at the smoothness of her warm skin. It made him want to slide his hand down under the collar of her blouse, but he resisted the urge. That might be taking friendship a little too far a little too fast.

The Shoreline Grill combined old-fashioned semiprivate booths with a modern menu that included mesquite-grilled meats and inventive pizzas. The manager hurried out and personally escorted them to one of his prime locations, with a view of the lake.

"It's good to see you again, Mr. Haley," he said, handing them menus. "We haven't seen you for quite some time."

"I haven't been going out much lately," Kane told him vaguely.

"Ah, but now, I'm sure we'll be seeing you again regularly," the manager said, giving Maggie a significant look.

He left before Kane could think of an answer to his insinuation, and for just a moment, both he and Maggie stared after the man, neither knowing what to say.

"Well, I guess…" he began.

"I don't think…" she began at the same time.

They both stopped, their gazes caught and then quickly detached again. Kane frowned. Things weren't working out quite the way he'd thought they would. He was feeling a strange awkwardness he wasn't used to, and he wasn't sure what was bringing it on. It seemed to have something to do with Maggie.

Probably because of his plan, he thought with a sense of relief that he'd pinpointed the problem. After all, it was manipulative. But necessary.

"Maggie," he said firmly, smiling at her in a friendly fashion. "We've worked together for a long time now. I think it's high time we put our relationship on a more personal level.''

''Oh no,'' she said, paling and looking positively dismayed at the thought. ''Let's not.''

It seemed an odd reaction, but he patted her hand in what he hoped was a reassuring manner. ''I'm talking about names, Maggie. I want you to call me Kane from now on. Except when we're in board meetings, of course. Things like that. But for the most part, you can call me Kane.''

''I don't think that's a very good idea,'' she said, ''I like it the way we have it. You're the boss and I'm the assistant. I can't call you by your first name.''

He stared at her for a moment. Had he ever noticed how blue her eyes were before? He couldn't remember. They sparkled like diamonds, making him wonder what she would look like all dressed up with fine gems draping down into that lovely cleavage.

But he shouldn't think that way about a married lady. And he shouldn't let himself get that tingle he was suddenly getting when he caught a hint of her spicy scent.

Shoving all that aside, he smiled at her. ''Come on. It's easy once you get used to it. Say *Kane*. You'll see.''

''No, I'd rather not.'' She pushed a strand of hair back into the twist at the back of her neck and he noticed, startled, that her fingers were trembling. ''Actually, I just think there's a lot of value in keeping the lines of responsibility clear. I like things in order. I like things to make sense.''

He stared at her for a long moment, strangely touched by how fierce her statement was, despite the fact that she was obviously very nervous. Was she afraid of him? That couldn't be. She'd faced him down in many a battle over work and he'd never noticed this trepidation in her before. It made him want to protect her.

They ordered lunch and once they were alone again, he cast about for some subject he could bring up that might get her mind off whatever was bothering her. The room was filled with customers. People-watching was always good for a comment or two.

"Look at that tall woman over there," he said, tactfully gesturing with his head and averting his eyes so that it wouldn't be obvious whom he was talking about. "The one in red. Do you see her?"

Maggie glanced up casually and looked back at him. "I see her."

He nodded knowingly. "I'd lay odds that she's pregnant," he said.

Maggie's mouth fell open with a slight gasp.

"I'm sure of it," he told her, gratified at her reaction. "I'd say almost five months along. What do you think?"

Her voice was choked when she answered. "I wouldn't know," she said. Reaching out for her glass, she took a huge gulp of ice water.

He glanced across the room again, then looked

back, smiling. "I'm getting pretty good at judging how far along the mothers are. It's becoming a real interest of mine. I can spot a pregnant woman across the room, even at about four months."

Maggie folded her hand primly in front of her on the table and tried to smile back. "Really?"

He leaned closer and went on earnestly. "Have you noticed that lately, there seem to be pregnant women around everywhere? It's like an epidemic or something. Every other woman I see is about to have a baby."

She seemed to swallow before answering, and then she turned her bright-blue eyes on him, looking puzzled. "I...I've got to admit, I've been having the same experience."

He nodded and muttered to himself, "See? It's not just me. I'm not going nuts."

But maybe she was. She shook her head as though to clear it. Too many things were coming at her too fast. She didn't know what to think any more. First there was the staring, then he'd asked her to call the clinic where she'd had her artificial insemination done. Then he'd made her come out to lunch with him, something he'd never done before, and now he was talking about babies and pregnant women. It was all too much. She felt as though she were out on a very high ledge and one misstep would send her plummeting into the void.

She took a deep breath, as though to steel herself, and looked him in the eye. "Mr. Haley, are you...?"

She stopped, then went on in a rush. "Are you...I don't know... in love or something?"

Her words went through him like an electric charge and he recoiled. "In love? Whatever gave you that idea?"

She shook her head and another strand of hair escaped the twist and curled in a gentle tendril in front of her tiny ear. "Well, you keep talking about babies, and..."

"Babies!" He glanced around as though to make sure no one had heard her. "Who said anything about babies?"

"You did, sir. And I think I'd better tell you..."

"Wait a minute." He glared at her. "I was not talking about babies. I was just trying to make conversation. And I'm definitely not in love."

"Oh." She sat back and pressed her lips together.

His glare lightened into a doubtful frown. "Why would I be talking about babies?"

She glanced up at him. "You said earlier that there was something magical about babies."

"It was just a common observation." His gaze sharpened. "Why would that make you think I was...in love?"

She shrugged, then looked at him searchingly. "Well, usually a man who is thinking about babies is planning to get married."

"Hah!" He nodded knowingly. "There's the problem right there. The marriage thing. That's where everything always goes wrong."

Maggie frowned at him. Her own marriage had been far from ideal, but she was definitely in favor of the institution. "What have you got against marriage?"

He paused while the waiter set a crab salad before Maggie and a steak sandwich in front of him.

"I've seen a lot of marriages," he told her, nodding the waiter away. "I know a thing or two about them." He took a bite of his garlic pickle and savored it as he thought over what he was about to say. "My uncle Joe, for instance, has been married seven times so far, and counting. And every single time, he's sure that this is the one, the true love of his life. The honeymoon is terrific. He's walking on air. And before the year is out, he's headed for divorce court. Again." He took a bite out of his sandwich as though he'd settled the matter for good.

She watched him eat through narrowed eyes. She couldn't let his opinion stand as though it were proven fact. "Have you ever considered that the flaw might reside in your uncle, and not the institution of marriage?" she asked him crisply.

"Of course. I'm not naive." He looked up and met her gaze.

As usual, that set off a tingle of reaction that she was beginning to wonder about. She could see that he was about to come back with something he obviously considered a zinger, but suddenly he hesitated. He seemed to remember that he was trying to charm her, not browbeat her, and he smoothly shifted gears.

"All this is just my opinion, of course. I know you're married, and for all I know, you may be quite happy with that situation. It seems to agree with you just fine. You're certainly blooming."

Maggie blinked. Two years a widow and he didn't know it. Well, that just about took the cake. It was beginning to look as if she wouldn't dare go on maternity leave. He wouldn't recognize her when she tried to come back.

Kane went on talking, but Maggie was having trouble following what he was saying. The food was delicious, but she couldn't eat more than a few tiny bites, and she spent most of her time pushing food around on her plate with her fork, hoping he wouldn't notice how little she was consuming.

She was getting very nervous. She had to find a way to tell him about her pregnancy. She'd tried once, but he hadn't let her get her sentence out. She had to do it. Now.

"Mr. Haley," she said when he'd paused for more than a few seconds. "There's something I really have to tell you."

"Say, look at the time," he said, glancing at his watch. "We'd better get back to the office. We still have that contract to get out before five."

She opened her mouth to try again, but he was already sliding out of the booth and reaching to help her. It was too late to do it now. Maybe back at work would be better anyway.

Chapter Three

But it wasn't. Once Maggie and Kane were back in the office there were a thousand things that had to be taken care of right away, and there was the contract, and the phone kept ringing. And all the time, the phrase beat like a drum at the back of her head— you've got to tell him, you've got to tell him.

But there didn't seem to be any time, and she was growing desperate. Any moment he was going to look at her and notice she was pregnant. After all, he was the expert, wasn't he? That almost made her laugh, but she held it back, knowing any laughter now would easily turn to hysteria. She had to get this done.

And then he cornered her in his office, and she knew it was too late.

"Maggie," he said, her name curling off his tongue in a way that made her shiver. "Come here and sit

down.'' He gestured toward the little couch against
the wall, near his floor-to-ceiling bookcase. ''I want
to talk to you.''

Her mouth was dry as she lowered herself to the
leather cushion. He'd noticed. She was sure of it. Oh,
why hadn't she had the nerve to tell him sooner?

He dropped down to sit beside her. Reaching out,
he took one of her hands and held it between his,
looking deeply into her eyes.

''Maggie, I'm glad we got to know each other better today,'' he said softly. ''That's very important to
me.''

She nodded, though she didn't know why. Heart in
her throat, she waited. Was this about her pregnancy
or not?

''Because now that we are…well, a bit closer,'' he
said, his eyes smiling. ''I feel that I can confide in
you.''

Not. This was something else. Her heart did a flip.
Something else. Something he wanted from her. What
on earth…?

''I would like to presume upon our fledgling friendship and ask you to help me with something very
personal.''

Oh my. She didn't like the sound of this at all.
''Mr. Haley, I don't think I'm the one for the job,''
she said so quickly, her words tumbled over each
other. She tried to pull her hand from between his.
''Really. I'm not too good at personal things.''

He smiled warmly, though he wouldn't let her hand

go. "You know, that's one of the attributes I like best about you. You're usually all business."

"Yes," she agreed, clinging to hope. "That *is* good, isn't it?"

"Usually. But right now, I've got a very big problem and I'm afraid I really need you to help me with it."

"Oh." Hope was fading.

"If it will help you to treat it like a business problem, why don't you do that? Take mental notes or whatever. Keep your perspective."

"I...I'll try."

"This is going to sound crazy. I can't really go into all the details right now and explain everything. You'll have to trust me. There's a logical explanation." He hesitated, then plunged on, staring earnestly into her eyes. "The fact is, someone in this building is pregnant with my baby. And I need your help to find her."

"Pregnant?" she whispered, stunned. Had she heard right? "How? I mean, wouldn't you know who she is?"

He shook his head. "Artificial insemination," he explained curtly. "It was a big mix-up. That was why I wanted to get in touch with the fertility clinic I asked you to call. It happened there."

"Oh."

The room was beginning to spin. It started very slowly, but she noticed right away. And at the same time, there was a strange buzzing in her ears. A funny little tune was playing in her head. "No, no, no, no," seemed to be the words.

"Maggie," he implored, holding her hand tightly. "I want you to know I've tried to do this on my own, but I've struck out every time. I really need your help."

"No, no, no," sang the little buzzing noise, and she realized she was holding her breath. What would happen if she let it go?

"You know a lot of the women here," he was saying. "I'm sure you could get a line on who she might be."

She tugged on her hand again, and he finally let it go, distracted by the plans he was making.

"Now, she should be about five months pregnant...."

She shook her head. This couldn't be happening. "No, no, no," she said softly, as though she could ward off the truth with the chant.

He looked at her strangely, but he was caught up in his agenda and didn't realize her reaction was so strong. He didn't seem to see that her eyes were slowly filling with tears.

"If you could just ask around, talk to some of the women you know, see what you can find out about anyone who might be five months pregnant...."

She sobbed. It came out involuntarily, like a big hiccup. He stopped dead and stared at her. She rose shakily from the couch. Tears were spilling from her eyes.

"Maggie," he said, surprise in his voice. He reached for her. "Why, what's wrong?"

The telephone rang. She turned as though to answer it, reacting automatically, and he let her go, though he followed her. She picked up the receiver and handed it to him without answering it herself. "It's for you," she said in a broken voice.

Confused, he took it and said, "Hello?" and before he could stop her, she was dashing from the room, and then onto the elevator and the doors were sliding shut.

Kane caught Maggie just before she reached her car. At first he thought she had herself under control again, but when she turned her tear-stained face up and he looked into the tragedy mirrored in her damp blue eyes and saw the way her lower lip was trembling, something skipped a beat near where his heart should be, and he felt an overwhelming urge to take her in his arms and comfort her.

"Maggie! What on earth?"

He resisted the impulse to pull her close, but he did take hold of her shoulders, holding her there and looking down at that beautiful mouth he was suddenly aching to kiss. Just for comfort, of course.

"Maggie, tell me what's wrong. Did I say something? Or do something?"

"No. No." She shook her head, her hair flying completely loose from the twist and spilling out over her shoulders. "It's...I've got to go. Please, Mr. Haley..."

She seemed to be afraid of something. Was it him? He couldn't stand the thought of it. He loosened his hold on her shoulders, caressing rather than gripping. And he tried to soften his face with a smile.

"Maggie, please. I have to know what's wrong. What did I do?"

"Nothing. It's nothing."

He reached for her chin, tilting it up in gentle persuasion. "You're going to have to tell me, you know."

"No. Mr. Haley...." She stopped, feeling trapped. It's none of your business. That was what she wanted to say. But she put her hand over her mouth because she was afraid it was very much his business. It was so much his business, she could hardly stand it. So she couldn't really say that, could she? Her huge blue eyes implored him.

"I have to go. I have to get home."

His long fingers curled around her fragile arms. "Why?"

She stared up at him. His face betrayed impatience, but his eyes shone with concern. It had to be done at some point. Why not now? She took a deep breath. "This is a terrible time to tell you, but I'm...I'm... I'm..."

She couldn't say it. Mute, she stared up helplessly and shook her head.

"You're what?" Frustration was beginning to take

its toll. "Sick? Angry with me? Bored with the job? Getting a divorce? What?"

She closed her eyes. "I'm pregnant."

There. It was out. She opened her eyes and looked at him.

His dark eyes were clouded, and she couldn't read a thing in them.

"Well," he said at last, speaking slowly. "I guess...well, congratulations."

"Thank you very much." She tried to peel away his fingers. "Now I've got to get home."

His grip on her only tightened. Maggie was pregnant. It probably had nothing to do with him. She had a husband, after all. And she was very unpregnant looking, so she couldn't be very far along. He would have noticed. So this had nothing to do with his situation, nothing at all.

"I suppose you're anxious to get home to talk to your husband about it," he said, his voice flat, his gaze probing hers.

She opened her mouth to tell him she had no husband, then closed it again. He noticed the gesture and a frown darkened his eyes, and then, quickly, a decision.

"Come on," he said, turning and forcing her to turn with him. "I'm driving you home."

"Oh, no! I can drive myself."

"No you can't. You're too upset."

Something was very wrong, and he was going to take care of it. If it had something to do with her husband, she might need him there as a backup. He didn't know why he was thinking along these lines. Some instinct was telling him to take care of her and that was what he was going to do.

They reached his silver Mercedes and he used his remote to open the doors. "My car is right here. Hop in."

"I'm fine," she protested, looking back down the parking structure at her own car.

"No, you're not. Get in or I'll pick you up and put you in."

She got in. "The contract!" she cried, turning to look at him as he slid into the driver's seat.

"Hell with the contract, Maggie. Your well-being is much more important than any damn contract."

Their gazes held for a long moment, and then she looked away. But it wasn't a surrender, and he didn't take it that way.

Still, he knew she was afraid of something. Was it her husband? Or something else? He didn't know, but he was going to take her home and assess the situation for himself. Right now, making sure Maggie was safe and secure was the most important thing.

Pulling out of the parking garage, he glanced at her sideways. Maggie was pregnant. He had to digest this, take it in and evaluate it. He was not going to jump to conclusions this time. He'd done that too often already with other women in his firm. It had been downright embarrassing when the truth had come out—that they each had perfectly rational explanations for their pregnancies that had nothing to do with him. He'd sworn he wouldn't get caught up in something like that again.

Besides, there was the husband. Was that what had her so upset? He'd brought up pregnancy and here she was, pregnant herself. Maybe her husband wasn't happy about it. Maybe there was something wrong with the baby. Maybe…

He glanced sideways at her and saw what he was looking for. She wasn't wearing a wedding ring. He remembered that she'd had one once. He'd noticed, because it had looked very much like the one he'd bought for his wife, Crystal, all those years ago. But it was gone now. His pulse began to race.

Don't be a fool, he told himself. It doesn't mean anything. A lot of women take off their wedding rings when they become pregnant. Sometimes it's because their fingers swell, sometimes it's because any kind of metal makes them itch during pregnancy. It's a funny time for a woman.

She gave him directions and they pulled into the parking garage of a high-rise apartment building.

"I'm coming up with you," he told her before she had a chance to dismiss him. "I want to make sure you're okay."

She stared at him for a moment, but she didn't ask why he thought she needed such help. Silently, she led the way through the security entrance, then up the elevator and on to her door, which she opened with her key. He followed her inside, looking about the room as though he expected to find something that would explain everything to him. He still had his car keys in his hand and he set them down on her dining table before turning to continue his scrutiny.

It was a modest apartment, in a building that had seen better days. She'd decorated nicely, but right now the bookshelves were only half filled, and cardboard boxes were strewn about, some full of household items, some empty.

"Are you moving?" he asked.

"Yes," she said. "I need a cheaper place. And they frown on children here."

He winced, remembering the times he'd complained about children in the courtyard of his old apartment, before he'd bought the penthouse he had now. Looking around again, he noted the absence of any sign of a masculine presence in the place.

"Maggie, you have to tell me the truth."

She looked at him pleadingly. "Do I?"

"Yes. Where's your husband?"

"I don't have a husband," she said, chin high and eyes clear now that she'd had a chance to settle down. "He died two years ago."

He took a deep breath. He'd thought as much. "Boyfriend?" he asked.

She shook her head.

He looked down at her stomach and frowned. "How far along are you?" he asked.

She started to turn away without answering, but he grabbed her arm. She felt so slim, so fragile, and his grip turned into more of a caress than anything else. Looking down into her tear-stained face, he repeated the question.

"You can't be five months," he said softly. "Can you?"

She looked up into his gaze and very slowly, she nodded.

"The Lakeside Reproductive Clinic?" he asked, his voice like ground glass.

She nodded again, her eyes shining bravely.

His heart was full, and he looked down into her beautiful face and did the only thing he could think of. He kissed her. A soft, quick kiss, lightly touching her lips, but to him, it sealed their new bond in a way nothing else could.

"We don't know for sure," she reminded him, drawing back. "Until Monday, when we can check with the clinic."

He nodded, and then he backed away from her a step or two.

He felt elated. The mystery was solved. He'd found his baby.

But at the same time, new questions were popping up everywhere, so many, his head was swimming. Maggie must have been feeling very similar doubts, because suddenly she was pressing his keys into his hand and guiding him toward the door.

"Go home and think this over," she told him. "On Monday, once we know for sure, we'll talk."

He lingered, reluctant to leave. "Are you going to

be okay?'' he asked. ''You have my home number, in case...''

''Go,'' she said, pushing him out. ''Just go.''

''Okay.''

He went and she closed the door behind him. He shoved his hands into his pockets and grinned. His baby was real. He'd found the little tyke. And he'd found his baby's mother. But as he made his way back down to his car, his grin faded. This wasn't the end of a quest. This was only the beginning. There was no doubt that his life was about to make a radical change. Was he ready for that?

Chapter Four

"So what do I do now?"

Kane hunched his shoulders under his rumpled suit coat and gazed at his brother across the kitchen table, his eyes intense, though bleary.

Mark yawned and shook his head. "Your guess is as good as mine," he said, pulling his robe more tightly against the cold morning air. The sun hadn't risen yet, but at least Jill, his wife, had coffee perking and breakfast started. "What do you *want* to do?"

Kane hesitated. He'd been in his car, out on the street, waiting for the first sign of life to come from Mark's house so he could knock on the door, for the last hour. He had to bounce his ideas off someone and he knew he wouldn't be able to sleep until he'd come to some sort of decision.

The minute the first light had flashed on, he'd been

at the front door with his finger on the bell, and he'd had most of his story out to his brother before they'd reached the kitchen. Now that Mark knew the essentials, he was hoping for a word or two of wisdom. But Mark had asked what he *wanted* to do. And that was just the problem. He wasn't sure.

"Okay, look," he said, leaning forward. "I've been thinking it over all night, and now I feel like I've got a hamster on a treadmill in my brain. I keep going over the same things, again and again. Give me something new. I need input."

Mark sat up straighter as Jill poured hot coffee into big mugs with large handles for each of them.

"I don't know what to tell you," Mark grumbled as he wrapped his hands around the steaming mug. "You wanted to know who was carrying your baby. Now you know. End of story."

Jill made a harrumphing sound as she set the coffeepot down on the counter, but neither of them noticed. She put a large frying pan on the burner and began breaking eggs into a bowl.

"I can't believe it's your administrative assistant," Mark said for the tenth time, shaking his head. "That's so weird."

"Maggie is anything but weird," Kane told him firmly. "You've met her. You know that."

Mark nodded. He and Jill had both met her at a few company parties they'd been invited to, but only fleetingly. "So where were you all night?" he asked with a grimace at Kane's crumpled clothing.

Kane leaned back, frowning as he tried to reconstruct his movements of the previous evening. "I stopped in at that little jazz club on Grand. Had a few drinks. Went to another club…"

"You drove in that condition?"

Their eyes met and a memory flashed between them. Kane knew they were both thinking about his father and his drinking problem. Though Mark had never known him, he knew all about the way alcohol had destroyed him. He and Kane never brought it up, but it was an unspoken piece of Kane's past that one had only heard of and the other had lived.

"No, of course not," Kane said quickly. "I took a cab at that point. And anyway, I didn't drink that much." He moved restlessly, pushing the mug from one place to another in front of him on the table. "So what am I going to do about this baby thing?"

Jill harrumphed again, and this time they both turned to look at her. She narrowed her cool green eyes, shook her headful of auburn curls, and sighed. Making a quick decision to join them, she turned off the burner under the eggs and sank down into a chair at the table. From the set of her shoulders, it was obvious she thought their conversation needed a little managing.

"Okay, Kane," she said, getting right to the point. "Here are your options. In the first place, you can walk away and ignore the entire thing. After all, she didn't ask you to get involved, did she? If you hadn't been doing the sleuthing, you probably wouldn't even know her baby was in any way related to you."

She paused to give him time to digest her words, and he frowned, slowly shaking his head.

"Okay, second option," she went on. "You can stay in the background but make sure she's always provided for. That gives her support but leaves you both free from an entangling relationship."

He didn't frown, but he looked uncomfortable, and she put her hand flat on the table with a decisive slap. "Or, you can do what's right," she announced firmly. "Step up to the plate and marry her,"

"Marry her!" Kane blanched, rearing back as though to get away from the very concept. "I can't get married. You know I've always said I never planned to get married again."

"Oh, come on," Jill said, her green eyes steady. "You never planned to have a baby, either. Life is what happens while we're making plans to do something else. But we deal with it."

Kane shook his head stubbornly, his dark eyes troubled. "No. No marrying. That's no good." His gaze met Jill's and then skittered away again. "I don't want all that upheaval that comes with marriage, and the unfulfilled expectations. I just want to be there for the kid if he needs me. I want to watch him grow up." He looked at Mark for understanding. "Do you get what I mean?"

Mark shrugged, looking wary.

Kane sighed and looked back at Jill. "I guess that

second option you were talking about comes closest to what I have in mind," he said reluctantly. "But I don't know...."

She hesitated, biting her lip as though not sure whether to give her own opinion, then gave into the impulse and reached out to take Kane's hand. "Okay, so you want to control her life and keep her nearby for your own reasons. Selfish, though understandable." She fixed him with a probing look. "But what are you giving her in return?"

He shrugged and answered a bit defensively. "A lot of money."

"Money!" Jill made a face, pulling her hand back. "Money is nothing!"

Mark looked hurt. "Thanks a lot," he said rather pathetically.

Jill reached out and squeezed his hand, too. "Oh, honey, you are a very good provider and we all appreciate it. But we could live under a bridge and still be a happy family, because of what else you bring to this enterprise. The money makes life easier, but it doesn't form the glue that keeps us together."

"No." He smiled at Jill, his eyes shining. "You do that."

They gazed into each other's faces like lovesick puppies, and Kane felt like snarling. Did they have to flaunt how happy their marriage was? He looked away, giving them a moment of privacy—kind of— then went on with his own problems. After all, that was what this meeting was supposed to be about.

"This is so messed up," he complained, sipping his coffee. "I thought that all I wanted was to find out who was having my baby. I had it all planned out in my head. I would be this smiling, benevolent person in the background, who would make sure the baby had a wonderful life, never asking for thanks or recognition…"

"Sort of a male fairy godmother," Jill broke in to offer, her eyebrows raised.

He gave her a baleful look, not sure if that was sarcasm he heard in her tone. "Sort of."

"Kane, honey, do you think a woman like your Maggie will go forever without getting married again?" she said softly. "I don't think so. She'll find someone eventually. And when she does, they'll be gone. They might move to California, for all you know. Japan. Tahiti. And what can you do about it?"

"That might be the best thing," Mark said, thinking he was being helpful. "I mean, if you just give her money and don't get involved personally, that leaves her free to form a new relationship and get a father for that kid."

Kane looked at them both in confusion. That kid. *That kid?* His kid.

"No." He was startled to hear himself say the word aloud.

"I am the father. I want to be his father." Was that really coming from his mouth? He wasn't even sure. Did he really want this? He'd never had a yen to have children before. Why was he feeling this way now?

"But you don't want to marry her." Jill threw out her hands, palms up. "Your choice, Kane. But without a marriage license, you have no control at all."

Kane's groan came from deep within his soul. "It all seemed so simple before I found out it was Maggie. Now that I know who it is…everything has changed. Nothing seems to fit together. There are too many questions." He gazed at them both, appalled. "This is crazy. I didn't realize that finding the answer would only open up a whole new can of worms. The decisions…the alternatives…the hopes and fears."

Mark and Jill looked at each other and laughed. "Welcome to parenthood," Jill said with due sympathy. "Hang on tight, honey. It's going to be a bumpy ride."

An hour later he was driving through the early-morning Chicago streets, still in a quandary. Mark and Jill had only managed to cloud the issues even further for him. What the hell was he going to do? He pulled over to the side, parking next to a bank of snow that had been shoved up out of the street, to give himself time to think.

He'd thought he'd had it all worked out, but now everything was so different from what he'd imagined—even more different than he'd let on to Mark and Jill. After all, Maggie was no unknown young woman married to a man whose privacy had to be respected. No matter how he might talk, this was not going to be a case of showing up once a year with goodies for the child and setting up a trust fund. This was his own Maggie who was going to have his baby, the woman who ruled over half of his life as it was.

He seemed to have known her forever, but that was just because she was so very important to him. Somehow he hadn't noticed as her influence over him grew and grew. Now he couldn't imagine life without her. He hadn't even begun to come to terms with what a difference that made.

He'd always liked her and certainly had respected her work. But now it was as if she'd been wearing a thick winter coat all these years—and had suddenly taken it off to reveal a very appealing womanly body underneath—something that had always been there, but hidden, waiting for the right moment. And now he was looking at her in a whole new light.

And that light was shedding more than illumination on the situation—it was laced with an erotic appeal that had been dormant but lurking beneath the surface all along. He thought of her sweet lips when he'd kissed her, and he took in a deep breath and held it. No, he could not walk away from this situation—but then, that had never been a real option. And since he had no intention of ever marrying again, that was no option, either. Which left…what exactly?

He had to decide. He was a man of determination and action and it was about time he showed it. Okay. By the time he got to Maggie's he would have his decision ready. And he would be prepared to handle the circumstances as they presented themselves. Setting his shoulders, he put his hands firmly on the wheel and began to drive.

Maggie hadn't slept much either. Her situation had become both dream and nightmare at the same time and she wasn't sure what she was going to do about it. After all, this was pretty scary.

How had this happened? She'd formed a deep desire, followed through on it, and now forces beyond her control were entering the picture. It was all so very spooky.

She had to admit that her dream of having a baby had included a shadowy donor father who looked a lot like Kane. She'd never once wished it were Kane himself. That would have been too contrary to the roles she saw them both in. Yet when she'd idealized that male part of the equation, it was definitely Kane's image looming in her heart.

But now the fact that her dream had come true was almost too close for comfort—as though it had all been preordained in some mystic, surreal manner. This wasn't the way she'd planned and imagined it. She hated to feel that the reins were slipping from her fingers.

Besides, it had never been a part of her dream that there would be a real live man in the picture. Real men brought along real complications. Her dream was of mother and child, the two of them together against the world. Though she was beginning to admit that dream was a bit unrealistic, she hated to let it go. It had kept her warm for so long....

When Kane buzzed her from the lobby, she knew who it was before she went to the receiver to answer his call.

"Who is it?" she said.

"It's me."

She swallowed and made a face. "I don't know anyone named Me,"

"Maggie, let me come up."

"It's so early."

"Or late," he said with the husky timbre of a man who hadn't had much sleep. "It depends on your perspective."

She sighed. He wasn't going to give up.

"All right," she said, and hit the release.

Then she looked at herself in the hall mirror and grimaced, pushing back the impulse to run for the bathroom and her makeup kit. This was the way she looked on Saturday mornings, hair in a braid down her back, baggy sweats and all. He might as well know the truth.

She started some coffee while she waited for him to come up to her floor, spilling grounds all over the counter. Exclaiming softly, she hurried to wipe up the mess.

She was nervous. A part of her was tempted to welcome Kane's involvement. After all, she'd been so all alone, and the more this baby had become a reality, the more she'd realized she'd begun a huge undertaking, and maybe, just maybe, she'd set herself up for disaster. To have someone on her side and in her corner, someone who cared right along with her…wouldn't that be wonderful?

She drew in a sharp breath and shook her head. Wonderful only in fairy tales. Real life had a way of turning on you. No, this was something she'd ventured into on her own and that was the way she wanted it to stay. She had to be strong.

Turning to wash out her dishrag, she knocked over a cup that she'd left beside the sink. Luckily, it was plastic and only bounced, but the fact that she'd done it didn't help her nerves at all, and she let out a cry that included a swear word she hardly ever used, then jumped when Kane's knuckles rapped on her door. Blood rushed to her cheeks as she wondered if he'd heard her curse.

She opened the door and got her answer.

"What's wrong?" was the first thing he said, feeding into her embarrassment.

"Nothing." She shook her head, avoiding his gaze. "Come on in," she mumbled, turning into the apartment, then turning back to look at him. There was something different about him this morning. It took a moment for her to realize what it was.

He looked happy. Really happy. Dread began to build in the area around her heart.

"Good morning," he said cheerfully, and his gaze went immediately to her stomach area.

"I just can't get over it," he said. "My baby.

You're nurturing my baby in there. It's like a miracle.''

She frowned at his words, but he didn't notice. He came on into her apartment, shedding his overcoat and turning to look at her as though he couldn't get enough of drinking her in.

She could tell right away that he hadn't been home yet. He needed a shave and his suit was rumpled, his tie gone and his shirt open at the neck. His dark hair looked ragged and a few strands fell over his forehead in an appealing manner. She'd never seen him look more gorgeous.

''A miracle,'' he said again with a reverence that surprised her.

And the baby must have heard him, because he took that moment to move inside, like a small earthquake. She put her hand over her stomach, suddenly feeling the wonder Kane was communicating to her. For just a moment, their gazes met and held, and her heart began to beat a rhythm that took her breath away.

She turned quickly, moving into her little kitchen. ''Coffee?'' she offered.

''Sure.'' He slid onto the bar stool at the counter and leaned his elbows on the surface. ''Meanwhile, I suppose you'd like to know just why this mix-up happened,'' he said dryly.

She looked up from pouring the coffee. It *was* something she'd been puzzled about. ''Tell me,'' she said.

He nodded and launched into a long explanation of how he'd accompanied his friend Bill when he was having his cancer treatments. Slowly, he edged into the sperm bank situation, staring down at his folded hands as he talked, trying to explain why he left a deposit of his own along with Bill's.

"I just don't understand," she said, bewildered. "I always thought of you as a clear-eyed businessman with a mind like a steel trap and a will to go with it. Why would you even do such a thing?"

He paused, trying to explain what had seemed so insignificant at the time. "It's like when my sister-in-law Jill is trying to get her toddler to eat his mashed peas. She says, 'Look, Kenny, they're so yummy!' And she takes a bite and smiles and pretends it's delicious, so Kenny will try it, too." He shrugged. "Bill was freaking out. He didn't want to do it. So when the technician suggested I go ahead and do it too, to put Bill's mind at ease, I was glad to help. I really meant to call back right away afterwards and tell them to destroy my sample. But it went flat out of my mind. I didn't think of it again until…it was too late." It all seemed too haphazard. At the time, it had seemed insignificant. And now, it meant everything.

Maggie listened, forgetting all about her beverage preparations, her heart thumping out a steady drumbeat in her chest. The whole situation seemed so wildly implausible.

"When they told me my…donation…had been used by someone in my own company, I was stunned," he said, looking up. "I went crazy trying to figure out who it could be. And when I found out it was you..."

She pulled her gaze away from the intensity of his and busied herself with the coffee again.

"Maggie, why were you having artificial insemination?" he asked softly.

She stopped what she was doing, steeled herself, and looked up into his eyes. "Because I want a baby so badly," she said in a clear, cool voice. "And I didn't want to remarry to have one."

She handed him his coffee and took a sip of her own. She knew he was puzzled by her answer, that he probably didn't approve. But he didn't say anything and she didn't offer any more explanation than that.

"What does your family think about it?" he asked.

"I don't have any family," she told him. "My parents have passed away. It's just me and the kid."

He half grinned at that. "You and the kid," he repeated softly. "And now there's me."

She didn't say anything. What could she say? That she didn't want him in her little family? That he was only an accident? No, that was too cold. Still, it was true.

"Okay, here's the deal," he said crisply, suddenly all business. "We'll go in Monday and find out for sure if our speculation is correct. But we both know it is. Don't we?"

She started to answer, but he went on without noticing, sliding off the bar stool and pacing the floor as he spoke.

"You'll quit your job at Kane Haley. And move into a very nice condo that's available in my building, just one floor down. I'll hire a truck and some packers to come take care of all this for you."

He waved at her half-packed boxes. "I don't want you bending and lifting. And I think it would be best if I hire someone to look after you all day, just in case. Hopefully someone who can take over being a nurse once the baby is born. Meanwhile, we'll start looking for a house for you in the suburbs."

She blinked at him. Here she'd been contemplating moving into a cheaper place that wasn't far from being a slum and economizing in every way she could. The future he laid out before her was a paradise compared to that. And he sounded so sure of himself. She felt a bit overwhelmed as he stopped and smiled into her eyes.

"Of course, we both want to do what's best for the baby. That will be my major concern in everything we plan from now on."

Of course. Important plans. The baby was the entire point. How could she not want what was best for him? She turned away and closed her eyes. Maybe he was right. After all, she was so all alone. Maybe it would be best to listen to him, to do what he said....

"I guess you're going to need some maternity clothes, aren't you? And I've got a friend who's an obstetrician. I'll get you an appointment right away."

Kane had it all planned out. How easy it would be to go along with him, let him make the choices, pay the bills, take control. All the worries, the struggling, would evaporate into thin air. She could relax and let him take over.

Suddenly a memory of Tom's face swam into her mind, his eyes cold, his mouth in a hard line of disapproval. She shuddered, pushing the image away. Turning, she stared at Kane. He was completely different from Tom. His face was so handsome, so kind. He wanted what was best for her, and the baby. That much was obvious.

"Here," he was saying, stopping at the counter and pulling out his check register and a pen and beginning to write. "I'll give you enough to cover any expenses you might have over the next few days." He ripped it from the book and held it out to her, his eyes warm, his mouth tilted at the corners in a smile.

"Maggie, this is going to be quite an adventure."

Her throat was dry. She picked up the check and looked at it. It was made out for a lot of money— more money than she made in a month. Her insides were shaking and she prayed her anxiety wouldn't show in her voice. She knew she had to maintain the iron discipline she assumed at work or she would melt into a quivering mound of Jell-O. And that couldn't happen. She couldn't let this relationship devolve into what she'd had before with Tom.

Looking up into his face, she tried to smile and

failed. "N-n-no," she said. "I can't." And she ripped the check in two.

Kane's face registered complete surprise. He looked at the torn pieces of paper in her hand and shook his head. "Maggie, what's wrong?" he said sharply.

She took in a deep breath and launched her defense. "Did it ever occur to you that this is an ongoing process, and you've come a bit late to the fair?" she asked him shakily.

The warmth had faded from his eyes and his brows began to move together. "I don't have a clue what you're talking about."

"Kane, I've been doing this for over five months. You just walk into the middle of things and expect to take over." She steadied her voice along with her breathing. It was coming easier now. "Why should you feel so free to change all the rules?"

He looked bewildered. "I'm not trying to change all the rules. I want to help you. I'm trying to get a handle on things...."

"You're trying to take control."

"What?"

His tone was less outraged than it was astonished, and she felt a pang of remorse for the stern way she was talking to him. But she knew it had to be done if she was going to maintain her position.

"The baby is mine," she told him, her voice still stiff, but softer now. "The baby may also be yours. Somewhat. And in that case, I'll be glad to have you as a male influence for my child. I admire you very much. But *I* will make all the final decisions for my baby.''

She steeled herself, expecting confrontation. Tom had always fought her every step of the way any time she tried to assert herself. She hated fighting. She usually tried to avoid it. That habit had led to Tom pretty much ruling their relationship. She couldn't let that happen here and she would fight if she had to.

But as she looked into Kane's eyes, she didn't see the anger she expected. She saw something else— something she didn't really recognize. And the next thing she knew, he was taking her hand in his and pulling her much too close.

''Maggie, does this have something to do with your husband dying?'' he asked her quietly, his dark eyes full of compassion for her position.

''My husband?'' She stared at him for a moment.

''You were so young to lose a husband you probably loved very much,'' he said, lacing his fingers through hers. ''I know you probably haven't gotten over losing him. Maggie, are you feeling that letting me get involved would somehow be disloyal to him?''

Her shoulders sagged and she wanted to laugh. If he only knew! ''Oh no, it's nothing like that.''

He drew her hand up and pressed it to his lips, searching her eyes for clues at the same time. ''You said there was no other man in your life.''

He was so close and so warm. She could feel his

body heat and it tickled her nose. How easy it would be to sink against him, let him hold her, let him make his plans for her life. Everything in her cried for that comfort.

"That's right," she said a bit breathlessly.

He smiled at her. "Then I'm going to be the man. You need one. And so does the...your baby." He shrugged, his dark eyes so very full of that sublime male confidence she could only envy and never hope to duplicate. "I don't see how you can stop me."

"Oh...I don't want to stop you...exactly. That's not it at all." How could she explain? He wasn't Tom, and yet, he was a man. She couldn't let him take over her life the way that men always did. She closed her eyes, trying to find a way to make him understand without making him into an enemy.

But before she thought of anything, he was releasing her, suddenly striding across the room, and she turned, surprised, to see what had caught his eye.

"Baby clothes?" he said as he dropped down into a squat to look into an open packing box. "You've already bought some baby clothes?"

Reaching in he pulled out a little blue shirt and held it up to the light, marveling at it. "Are they really this small?" he murmured, rising and turning toward Maggie, his face glowing.

"Newborns are even smaller," she said.

He looked down at the shirt again, imagining a tiny, squirming body inside it. Then he realized what the color meant. "Do you already know the gender?" he asked her hopefully.

Despite everything, she smiled. She couldn't help it. How seductively delightful to have someone to share the joy with. "Yes. It's a boy."

"A boy." His heart was so full, he had to turn away so that she wouldn't see his eyes misting. "A boy." He could barely stand to stay calm. He remembered himself with his own father. And he also remembered his devastation when he'd lost the man. How his mother had begun going off to work every day and leaving him with sitters. How he'd waited for a father who never came home again.

Actually, once he'd become an adult and had looked into the facts of the matter, he could see that his mother hadn't waited all that long to remarry and supply him with a father again. But, as much as he'd liked his stepfather, he'd always thought of him as a visitor. He'd always been waiting for his own father to finally come home again. Sometimes he felt as though he were still waiting.

He turned to look back at Maggie. He liked the way her hair was escaping from the braid at the back of her neck, liked the way her breasts looked under the soft cloth of her sweatshirt, liked her feet in fuzzy socks. He wanted to put his arms around her and hug her close.

But they didn't quite have that sort of relationship. She would think it odd if he did it. She might even push him away.

Still, it was time to make some sort of statement. He took a deep breath, and then he told her how he felt.

"I think I know what we're going to have to do," he said.

She gazed at him in surprise. "What is that?"

"I think we're going to have to get married," he said. "I know that wasn't in your plans. But hey, life messes up our plans all the time." That wasn't quite the way Jill had put it, but it would have to do. "Yes, we'll have to get married." And then he shrugged happily. "There's just no other way."

Chapter Five

The verdict was in. Suspicions confirmed. Everything was official.

Kane and Maggie came back from meeting with the people at the fertility clinic, riding up in the elevator as silently as they'd spent the last half hour in the car together. They walked into Kane's office without a word, sat down across from each other at his desk, and stared into each other's eyes.

Kane swallowed hard. He'd known it was true, and yet, having it corroborated stunned him all over again. Somehow fate had stepped in and taken charge of their lives. Somewhere a mischievous angel had to be laughing his head off.

"Well," he said, frowning slightly, not sure what to say next.

"Well," Maggie echoed, her eyes filled with a vaguely bewildered expression.

Kane shrugged, then reached across the desk and grabbed her hand in his, holding tightly. "Do you realize what this means?" he demanded, looking into her eyes with an intensity that startled her. "Do you get it? No matter what we do—no matter where we go from here—you and I are locked together *forever.*"

She stared at him. It was almost too big a thought to encompass at the moment. Forever. No matter what. Forever. Their shared future seemed to stretch into infinity.

"You see?" he said softly, his eyes shining. "We might as well get married."

"Oh!" She pulled her hand back and gave him a look of exasperation mixed with apprehension. "Enough with the marriage talk!"

He leaned back in his chair, but he wasn't giving up. He wanted to marry her. He'd been trying to get her to see things his way since Saturday morning and he wasn't used to being denied. He was sure it was only a matter of time before he convinced her. After all, he'd convinced himself, and if anyone had ever been standing firm against marriage, he was that man.

The problem was, the argument that had turned him around wouldn't work on Maggie. Whenever he wavered, Jill's words echoed in his mind.

Without a marriage license, you have no control at all.

He knew enough from his experience in business to know that his sister-in-law was absolutely right. Without a seat on the board, you had no say in the destiny of the company. Without a marriage license, he would have no say in the destiny of his child.

Case closed. *One marriage license to go, please.*

"Maggie," he said quietly, watching her reaction. "We're parents. Everything will work out much better if we become partners as well."

She risked a quick look into his eyes, then looked away again. "We're already partners," she said stubbornly. "Why do we need a piece of paper from the government to ratify it?"

"Because we have a baby coming."

She closed her eyes, letting her head fall back, then roused herself and rose from the chair, going to pick up a file from atop his desk and carry it over to his handsome oak file cabinet. Pulling open the drawer, she found the place where the file belonged and shoved it into the slot, then pushed the drawer closed again.

Turning, she looked around for something else to tidy up. The darn place was too neat. As a last resort, she finally looked down at Kane, still sitting in his desk chair, watching her every move.

"Can't we just go on as we have?" she said, clutching one hand with the other and talking a little too fast. "I'm so happy working for you. We really get along well in this office. We're...we're already like a team of sorts. I feel right and sure of what I'm doing here.'' She leaned closer, beseeching him with her beautiful eyes. "Can't we just keep doing that?"

When she looked at him like that, her clear and sparkling gaze so full of emotion, her lower lip just a bit swollen, holding herself so unselfconsciously, he wanted to give her anything she wanted. But this was one case where he couldn't do what came naturally. He wasn't looking forward to what he would see in her eyes when he told her that. Steeling himself, he did what he had to.

"We can't, Maggie. It's impossible. You're having a baby. Everything has changed."

She spun away from him and began to pace the floor of his office, feeling the way a caged cat must feel. The walls were closing in. He was slowly trapping her and she knew it. But she wasn't ready to admit defeat. Not yet.

"We can fit him in," she said hopefully. "I can work right up to my due date, and afterwards, I could bring him to the office with me. The day-care center should be up to speed by then, and..."

"The day-care center." He sighed heavily, turning away as though annoyed by the thought. "You can't count on the day-care center."

She frowned at him. "Why not? I thought..."

He waved the topic away, rising and coming toward her. "Anyway, that's a completely naive scenario and you know it. Things can't go on the way they have been. The child changes everything."

Yes, of course. He was right. The child changed everything. Why hadn't she seen this coming?

But she *had* seen it, and she'd just pushed the knowledge aside. She'd wanted a baby and she wouldn't let good sense shake her out of it. She'd wanted what she wanted, with a longing so intense, she'd gone a little nuts.

How could she explain that to Kane? How could she make him see that her baby was so important to her—so important that she couldn't let control slip away? She couldn't very well tell him that she didn't want to marry him because she wanted her baby all to herself. It was too late for that.

"Naive" he'd called her. And he was right. She kept making impulsive decisions and ignoring the consequences that were so obvious to anyone else. Was she doing that again by turning him down?

"Things can't go on as they have," he reminded her. "Things will change. They have to."

"Yes," she said softly.

"And so, what is it that you want?" he asked her. "What do you see as the way we should handle this?"

He was standing very close and she was in danger of losing perspective. He'd always made her dizzy when she'd been near enough to catch the fragrance of his aftershave, but that casual hint of vertigo was morphing into a high that threatened disaster if she didn't move away. She gazed up at him, knowing she must look like a space cadet.

"I think I need time to figure that out," she said as firmly as she was able.

"Time is the one thing we don't have a lot of," he said, and suddenly she was in his strong arms. "Let's get married."

"We can't," she said breathlessly, her hands flattened against his hard chest. The sense of strength and maleness was so potent, her head was swimming, but she had to keep her wits about her and stick to the subject. She desperately cast about for a good reason to give him, something he might listen to. "Kane, look...we don't love each other."

The embrace that had begun turning her bones to mush evaporated, and he stepped back, away from her. "No, we don't love each other," he agreed, his voice colder now. "I never said we did."

She searched his dark gaze. She'd wanted to stop his seduction, but she hadn't meant to wound him. Why did she get the impression he'd been hurt by what she'd said? It was only the truth. Surely he didn't think...?

"We don't love each other," he said again, and now his voice was calm and quite casual. Maybe she'd imagined what she'd thought she heard. "But we like each other pretty well," he went on. "Don't we?"

"I think so."

"And we both have the same goals. We want this child and we want what's best for him."

"Yes."

He dropped onto the surface of the desk, hooking his leg over the corner and folding his arms across his chest. "Look, Maggie. I married for love the first time. Or what I thought was love. And it didn't work out well at all."

She nodded. She certainly understood how that could happen. "I'm sorry."

"The woman I thought would make my life a heaven on earth turned my existence into a living hell." He stopped himself, making a face. "It wasn't actually quite as dramatic as that sounds. But love disappeared as soon as we got to know each other better and our egos began to clash. So don't tell me how important it is to love. Love is like icing on the cake. You can get along fine without it if the cake itself is full of enough goodies."

Despite everything, she had to laugh at that one. "And you think we've got enough goodies to throw into the mix?" she asked him.

His lopsided grin was her answer. And then there was something more in his eyes and that electric thing flashed between them again and she quickly looked away.

"How about you?" he asked as she went back to pacing before him. "Did you marry for love?"

She spun and braved another full look into his face. "Of course."

"And did it turn out the way you'd thought it would?"

She turned her head and bit her lip. "That's not the point."

"It's exactly the point. Maggie, love is a volatile emotion. It goes up like a flame and dies just as suddenly."

She frowned. She didn't like what he'd just said, didn't want to believe it, despite her own experience. It was just too cynical. If you couldn't hope for the redeeming magic of love, what could you hope for?

But he was going on.

"We've worked together for two years. We know we get along fine."

He rose from the desk and took hold of her shoulders, forcing her to look into his eyes. "Hey, nothing can stop us. We can do this." He smiled at her. "All we need is the will."

No, she needed a lot more than that. She needed guarantees.

And she needed not to feel all quivery inside whenever he touched her like this.

The telephone rang and she jumped at this reminder that they were in a business office in the middle of the business day. Kane reached out and answered it and she took the opportunity to start back toward her own desk. But he put the call on hold and called out to her.

"Maggie, wait a minute. We've got to establish our plans. How long do you need?"

She stared at him for a moment, not sure she knew what he meant. "Why do we have to...?" she began.

"Because people are going to begin noticing your condition," he said a bit impatiently. "Whatever we decide to do, don't you think it would be best to do it before they begin to talk?"

He was right, of course. By the end of the week, she would have to have a plan.

"Friday," she told him quickly. "I'll decide by Friday."

He nodded, his dark eyes hooded. "Okay. 'Til Friday."

Maggie had a doctor's appointment on Thursday. She'd toyed with letting Kane come along to meet her doctor, but at the last minute she'd decided against it.

"Don't you think I should be involved in these things?" he'd said when she told him.

She gave him a long-suffering look. "Involved in what? Having your blood pressure checked? Testing for diabetes? Consulting on your diet? Finding out how to avoid swollen ankles?"

He looked pained. "Well..."

She put a hand on his arm. "Of course you should come and meet the doctor," she told him. "When we get things settled and know where we're going, you'll want to come and hear how things are progressing directly from him. But not yet."

She'd noted the rebellious light in his eyes, but she didn't relent. She had a few more questions she wanted to ask, a few things to go over with the obstetrician, before she brought Kane along.

The funny thing was, now that she was tidying up her desk and getting ready to leave, he seemed almost anxious to get rid of her.

"Isn't it getting late for your appointment?" he asked, leaning against his doorway and making a show of glancing at his watch. "You don't want to get stuck in traffic and miss it."

"Don't worry. It's only a few miles away." She rose from her desk. "I've got Hannah and Kate covering the phones for you," she told him. The two secretaries were in the adjoining office, near enough to call for help when they were needed, but partitioned off so that they weren't in the way at any other time.

She gathered her things, put on her coat, then looked back to find him still waiting for her to leave.

"What's the matter?" she asked him. He looked so enticingly tall and lean, propped against the doorjamb the way he was, and yet something about the manner in which he was looking at her made her want to laugh. He reminded her of a little boy hiding something behind his back.

"The matter?" He was all innocence. "Nothing. Nothing at all." He smiled at her. "Get going. Give me a call if you have any problems."

"I will." She gazed at him suspiciously for another moment, then shook her head and turned to leave.

Once alone in the elevator, she closed her eyes and laughed softly.

"Oh, Kane," she whispered. "What are you up to?"

It was amazing, really, how much their relationship had blossomed in so short a time. Maggie had always thought that she loved working for Kane—loved the atmosphere of the office, loved the hustle and bustle and the responsibility. The rapport between the two of them had made it all special. They had such a good relationship, close enough to feel attached, reserved enough to feel independent. There was dignity in that. Pride. A sense of mutual respect. For a long time, she'd thought things were about as good as they could get.

But she knew now that she'd been wrong. Things had become a little crazier. But they were better. Despite the fact that she was often on tenterhooks, wondering what she should do, there was also a new affection between them that filled her with a warmth she'd never known before. And the thought of having him around to support her was such a relief.

As she walked through the parking structure to where her car was parked, she admitted to herself what she'd come more and more to realize—that she'd had no business trying to do this on her own. The nuclear family was the basic building block of civilization for a very good reason—it worked. A mother and a daddy and a child—there were those who managed it without all those essential ingredients, but it would be very tough. And why had she been so determined to make this harder than it had to be? She had such a good man wanting to help—a man who was going to be around anyway, no matter what she did.

The one fear that still shook her was a deep and private one. Things seemed promising now, but— would he change the way Tom had changed? The more she thought about it the more she knew there had been signs of how Tom would transform himself from a loving, attentive boyfriend to a cold, manipulative husband—signs she'd ignored. She didn't see any of those signs with Kane. But maybe there were others. Was she just ignoring warning signals again? Did she purposely blind herself to things she just didn't want to see? She didn't have the greatest track record. How could she know for sure?

Kane waited about five minutes, drumming his fingers on the surface of his desk and watching the clock. When he'd finally decided she'd had enough time to be in her car and on her way, he sprang into action. The first thing he did was call CeCe in the mailroom.

"Okay," he said. "She's gone. You can bring the stuff up now."

Clicking off, he looked around the office suite with a smile. He'd never paid the slightest bit of attention to Valentine's Day before. Chances were he probably wouldn't ever pay much attention to the holiday again, unless forced to. But for some reason, he'd gone all out today.

Reaching into the area under his desk, he pulled out a large stuffed penguin, very plush, with a large red, embroidered Be Mine heart on its chest. He plopped it down in Maggie's desk chair and gazed at it, satisfied. It looked as though a rather short, good-natured man sporting a tuxedo was filling in for her.

"Very cute," he muttered to himself. "Women love cute."

The penguin seemed to nod in agreement, and Kane moved on to the elevator, arriving just in time to meet CeCe and her part-time assistant Brandon Levy as the doors slid open. The short, dark woman was pushing a cart filled to the brim with items chosen to change the area into a hearts-and-flowers wonderland, and the young man was along for the ride but looking suspicious about the whole affair. Kane took one look at the two of them and went into military mode. This was a rather large operation and it would take strategy and leadership to get everything into place in time.

"Okay, CeCe," he said briskly. "Just wheel it on in here. The flowers go on this table. We'll divide them up between these four vases. The balloons we'll attach to her desk by the strings with this tape dispenser. The candy goes in these little glass dishes shaped like hearts. Brandon, you can get going on those. The banner goes over the entryway. And the paper and Mylar hearts go every damn place you can find to stick them.''

CeCe pushed the cart into the area he'd indicated and began unpacking all the items he'd secretly hidden in her mailroom over the last few days.

''Aye aye, Boss,'' she said pertly, doing just as she'd been told, but giving him a few sideways glances when she thought he wasn't looking. Her curiosity was obvious. She finished unpacking her cart and began arranging the flowers in vases as she watched him put up the banner and then begin work on the balloons. Finally, she couldn't hold back a question.

''Is there…some sort of an official reason for this little celebration?''

His gaze was cool and not the least bit welcoming. ''I don't know what you're talking about,'' he said as he taped another batch of balloons to the cardboard blotter on Maggie's desk. ''It's Valentine's Day, isn't it? Isn't everyone doing something like this?''

''Like this, no,'' she murmured, barely concealing her grin. She set one of the flower arrangements on the file cabinet beside Maggie's desk, leaned back to check it out, then turned to talk to Kane again, her head to the side. ''I take it this is a whole new phase in your life.''

''CeCe,'' he said impatiently, accidentally popping one of the white balloons and swearing under his breath. ''You're not making any sense.''

She grinned at him openly now. ''Falling in love

with love they call it, don't they?'' She pretended to give him an elbow to the ribs. ''What happened to old Mr. Cynical?''

''He's still here,'' Kane retorted grumpily, taking a step back out of range of her elbow. ''This is just for Maggie. She deserves a little something special.'' He glared at her. ''And you don't have to make any more out of it than that.''

''Who, me?'' CeCe's eyes were big as saucers. ''My lips are sealed.''

''And so will your fate be if you don't keep this under your hat,'' he warned.

''Wow, threats!'' she teased. ''This must be serious.''

He turned and looked at her, his mouth twisted. ''Ever been to Siberia?'' he asked. ''I can get you assigned to a nice little mailroom there. I've got connections.''

CeCe rolled her eyes. ''You belong on a slow boat to China if you think you can keep this story under wraps,'' she told him. ''I'll bet it's already all over the building.''

''How could it be? We haven't even finished decorating yet.''

''Oh, I don't know. These things take on a life of their own.''

He gazed at her with suspicion, but she smiled blithely and prepared to take her assistant and her cart back down to the mailroom. He went back to taping hearts up and soon he was alone with a beautifully decorated office, if he did say so himself.

He turned slowly, taking it all in and feeling a sense of accomplishment such as he hadn't felt in years. He'd never done anything like this before, and he thought it had turned out pretty well.

Now it was time for the pièce de résistance. Going back to his desk, he took out a card and slipped it from its envelope. It hadn't been easy finding one that held enough sentiment and yet didn't talk about love. He'd finally settled on a beautiful flower on the outside and the simple words, "Valentine's Day is for loving hearts" on the inside. Under the printed message he wrote,

Both our loving hearts have been stolen by one baby.

Let's do life together. It seems like the right thing to do.

He put the card back in its envelope and placed it in front of the penguin on her desk. Then he went back to his own desk and sat down to wait. How long did a checkup like this take, anyway? He had no idea. But he knew he wasn't going to get any work done until she was back. So he waited.

And waited.

He got a little work done, but he spent most of his time checking the clock and looking up every time the elevator dinged.

Funny, but there seemed to be more traffic than usual today. The only other attractions on this floor were a pair of conference rooms and a corporate library where research could be done and business archives consulted. None of them were much used, and yet small groups of women were coming by regularly, whispering and giggling as they took in the decorations. It was beginning to get annoying. He felt like a destination on the city tour, right along with the Water Tower and the Hancock Building.

"CeCe, you're going to pay for this," he muttered, though he knew it was an empty threat. He just didn't have quite the old iron will he used to exhibit around here. Who would have believed he would end up decorating for Valentine's Day? No wonder they were coming up to take a look as though he were a circus freak. He was!

He sat back in his chair starting to feel a bit morose. What the hell was he doing, anyway? Ever since he'd found out he had a baby, he'd been acting like a man with a personality transplant. And then, when Maggie was thrown into the brew—all hell had broken loose inside his soul. Lately it was as though he was a different person—as if mouth-breathing aliens had seized control of his brain. He was clumping around like some lovesick Neanderthal, bumping into walls and saying stupid things. He was even trying to get Maggie to marry him. Marry him!

He'd once sworn he would never marry again. His marriage to Crystal had been a disaster. Willowy tall and smooth as silk, she'd seemed the most beautiful woman in the world to him at the time. She'd also turned out to be the greediest and pretty high on the dishonesty scale as well. She may have married him for love, but she stuck around for the loot, and when that didn't pour out quite as generously as she'd expected, she took off for greener pastures.

He knew there were good relationships in the world. He saw his brother and Jill and what they had together. And actually, his mother's marriage to Mark's father had been pretty happy. So why did he have, in the depths of his soul, this conviction that marriage was a sham?

He'd tortured himself with these questions for years and finally decided it must be him. Everyone seemed to disappoint him in the end. Nobody stuck around to see things through. Deep inside, he was always that little boy, waiting for his father to come home and knowing, with the clear sight of the often disappointed, that he never would again.

And so here he was, ready to try married life one more time. He knew from experience that a marriage license wouldn't stop anyone from walking out. But being married when the baby was born would give him a lot more leverage. He'd be the father of record in every way. There would be no room for doubt. And a child couldn't walk out on you. At least, not until he was eighteen.

Maggie knew something was different the moment she drove into the parking structure. The guard who usually waved her in with a stiff smile had a big grin instead, a grin that looked just a little too personal.

"Hi, Mrs. Steward," he said. "Back so soon?"

"Yes," she said, gazing at him curiously. He seldom spoke to her this way. "Why? Has something happened?"

"Oh, no," he said, but the glint in his eye said otherwise.

Maggie parked and went into the building. Trudy, the receptionist in the main lobby, looked up with a know-it-all smirk.

"Good afternoon, Maggie," she said, eyes dancing with mirth.

"Hello, Trudy," Maggie said, turning to look at her again as she waited for the elevator. The woman had never so much as raised a painted eyebrow at her before. What on earth was going on?

Two women she didn't know were behind her in the elevator. She smiled at them as she got on, then turned and felt the silence, pregnant with suppressed whispering, behind her, knowing their gazes were riveted to her back. The hair was rising at the nape of her neck. They had been talking about her before she got on and would continue to talk about her once she was out of earshot. She knew it as though she'd been officially informed.

The elevator stopped at the thirteenth floor and the two women got off, glancing back at Maggie as they did so. Lauren Mitchell, one of her favorite secretaries, was walking by in the hallway and caught sight of her.

"Hi Maggie," she called. "Happy Valentine's Day!" She waved and Maggie waved back.

"Same to you," she said as the doors began to close. Was it her imagination, or did Lauren start to laugh?

Valentine's Day. She'd forgotten. There had been some decorations here and there around the offices, but the employees at Kane Haley usually didn't make a big deal of Valentine's Day—at least, not that she'd ever noticed before. Or maybe she'd just ignored it because she'd known she wasn't going to get a special card or gift from anyone.

Still, it being Valentine's Day couldn't account for the crazy way people were acting toward her. She wished she could figure out what was going on.

The elevator stopped at the next floor, and since there didn't seem to be any reason for it, Maggie pushed the Close button, but before she could get going, she noticed that people were sticking their heads out all up and down the cubicle row and the murmur seemed to be along the lines of, "There she is! That's her."

She stared out at all the interest. Her cheeks were coloring. Suddenly she noticed CeCe just a few feet away with her mail cart. CeCe was shaking her head, looking worried.

"Hi, Maggie," she cried anxiously. "It wasn't me, I swear."

"What are you talking about?" Maggie demanded.

"Don't blame me," CeCe cried.

The doors closed before Maggie could ask again.

The elevator doors opened at her floor and she gasped. The entire office suite was awash in streamers and fluttering hearts. Red and white balloons looked about to carry away her desk. Red and white carnations filled the air with perfume. And a huge banner said "Happy Valentine's Day" in red velveteen lettering.

"Oh no," she moaned, her hands to her face. No wonder the entire building was buzzing. This was terrible. Why hadn't he just taken out a full-page ad in the local papers? Why hadn't he put up a neon sign across the front of the building? What was he thinking?

"Kane," she wailed, and suddenly, there he was, pushing aside a bevy of balloons and coming toward her. "What on earth…?"

"Hey, Sugar," he said, holding out a velvet-covered heart filled with expensive chocolates. "Happy V-day. Did you know I'm sweet on you?"

She stared at him. What could she say? His eyes were full of humor, but also a certain expectation. He wanted her to love this. And…well, what the heck? Why shouldn't she? She looked around at all the white lace and red ribbons. And suddenly, she did love it. No one had ever done anything like this for her before.

Laughing along with him, she turned slowly, gazing at it all in wonder, lingering particularly on the plush penguin who seemed to be winking at her.

"What is this?" she cried.

"A Valentine's party. Can't you tell?"

She turned to look at him. "I never knew you to be so into holidays before," she said, careful to keep things impersonal.

He smiled and took back the candy, setting the box on the desk, before taking her into his arms, holding her loosely.

"Have dinner with me tonight. I've got reservations at Le Jardin."

"Oh, but…"

"No backing out."

She sighed. His eyes were bright with affection, but it wasn't the least bit threatening. She felt herself begin to relax. "Well, it would be fun," she admitted.

He nodded, satisfied and pulled her a little closer.

"And now, we need to kiss," he announced, as though it were the most natural thing in the world.

"Says who!" she demanded, putting her hands on his chest in defense.

He gazed at her, all wide-eyed innocence. "It's traditional. Like under the mistletoe."

"That's Christmas," she scoffed, but she was laughing.

"This is a new tradition. I'm starting it right now. A Valentine's kiss."

"Oh Kane, I don't know…"

"I do."

It was supposed to be a sweet kiss, a friendly reminder of the ties that held them together, nothing scary, nothing particularly sensual. She knew that was what he meant to do. She saw it in his eyes, felt it in his voice. But something happened neither of them had expected.

As his lips touched hers, her mouth opened as naturally as a flower opens to the sun. He was so warm and he tasted like wine and springtime and something dark and arousing and just a little scary.

All thought faded to make way for feeling and every part of her body wanted to touch him, to curl around him, take him in—devour him as though she were a starving thing that needed him to survive. And deep inside her, a smoldering fire ignited, burning its way into her soul.

"Oh!" she cried, jerking back away from him in horror at her own sudden surge of desire.

His eyes were smoky, but she couldn't tell what his response really was. His wide mouth curved in a smile as he still held her, but only by the shoulders.

"Whoa," he said. "I guess we'd better not do *that* again."

What did he mean? Had he felt the same way she had? Or was he just remarking on how she'd gone all romantic on him? She swallowed hard, her gaze held by his, feeling queasy and knowing that there was going to be no cure for what she'd come down with. Her only hope was going to be to stay as far from

Kane as she could get. And how did you do that when you were married?

She turned away from him and remembered something. Looking back at him with a tremulous smile, she said, "I have a Valentine for you, too." She reached into her purse and pulled out the sonogram picture the doctor had given her, taken that very afternoon. "Actually, it's from both of us." She held it out to him. "Here's your baby."

It was the first time she'd said that, the first time she'd really acknowledged just what this child was in such a straightforward way. And the look on Kane's face as he took the picture and looked at it told her that what she'd done meant everything to him. She melted. How could she not love that reaction?

Chapter Six

Dinner at Le Jardin was lovely. They ordered sautéed Chilean sea bass with saffron lobster broth and listened to Edith Piaf songs sung by a rail-thin woman in a striped jersey shirt and a black beret.

"Isn't this romantic?" they heard a passing woman say to her companion in reaction to the vocalist. "Like Paris in the forties."

Maggie had to laugh, leaning across the table to muse softly to Kane, "She's right, you know. But why is it romantic to be reminded of the Second World War?"

He grinned at her, then sobered thoughtfully. "Maybe because it was a time when people knew what they believed in and knew what they were fighting against. There were no doubts, no second thoughts."

Maggie gave him a skeptical look. "I'll bet they weren't really that much different from the way we are now."

"Maybe not. But that's the image we have of that time. And we all long for a little more certainty in our lives. Don't we?"

She nodded in agreement. "No doubts," she murmured, her eyes glazing over for a moment. Yes, that would be nice.

The sommelier brought the wine and poured out a bit for Kane to taste. She watched him as he concentrated on his task. He looked so right doing it. This was where he belonged, where he knew his way around instinctively. He was so handsome in the candlelight, the shadows playing on his high cheekbones, the flame striking sparks in his eyes. He was the portrait of the perfect gentleman from the elite of his society.

The next thought that struck her was, What am I doing in this picture?

Kane was a wonderful man. She'd always known that. And now she also knew that he was warm and affectionate and fun to be with. She couldn't help but think how much happier life could be with a man like Kane in it—if only...

It was too bad he didn't love her. She knew that—after all, they'd worked together closely for two years and he'd never once thought of her romantically—not for one moment. Things had changed now, of course. But only because of the baby. He wanted his child.

And she couldn't blame him. She wanted that child as well.

He was nodding his approval of the wine, and then he looked up to meet her scrutiny. His dark eyes sparkled. "Would you like to dance?" he offered quietly, leaning toward her.

"Dance!" She repeated the word a little too loudly in her surprise, because she had never even considered dancing with Kane and the prospect was daunting—but her word came across as though she thought he'd suggested she do it by herself and on top of the table to boot. Even the sommelier, busy pouring her glass of wine, couldn't resist a snicker and Kane laughed right out loud.

Her face felt hot, and the next thing she knew, he was leading her onto the little dance floor. The Edith Piaf impersonator had vanished and a small combo was playing sultry music that made Maggie think of small boulevard cafés where French artists with smoldering eyes danced with lovers who held knives in their garters, late into the steamy nights.

This night was hardly steamy. But her emotions were certainly beginning to simmer. And when Kane drew her close she stiffened, afraid to let him see how his nearness made her feel.

But it was no use. His warm breath was stirring the hair around her ear. If she closed her eyes, she could hear his heartbeat. Or was that her own? She wasn't sure. She only knew it was beating out a rhythm much more insistent than that of the music, and that listening too long could drive her to the edge of sweet insanity.

She closed her eyes and let the music take over, let herself melt against him. If she could forget that she was pregnant, if she could float in a fantasy of "no doubts, no second thoughts"—if she could pretend that Kane might love her someday—she could let herself relax and enjoy this.

The music stopped, but he was still holding her. She looked up and her eyes met his. There was something dark and stormy in his gaze, something that seemed to be reaching for her in a spiritual way that almost scared her.

And then she realized what it was. He wanted her. The dance, their closeness, had revealed a desire she'd never thought she'd see in him. Her breath caught in her throat and her heart began to race.

"Come on," he said huskily, his warm hand at the back of her neck to guide her. "They're probably ready to serve us something to eat by now."

She looked at him, his smile bland and casual. But she was sure of what she'd just seen. He had wanted her. Unless she was crazy. Unless she was fooling herself again.

They sat back down at their table and ate. Each dish was more delicious than the last. They chatted while they ate, laughing softly about anecdotes they took turns relating to one another. Once they'd finished the meal, they sat on, listening to the Edith Piaf singer again and drinking very black coffee out of tiny porcelain cups.

And then Kane leaned close and said softly, "You're still resisting this marriage thing, aren't you?"

"Kane..."

He held up a hand. "Just a moment now. I can feel that you are. I only have a short time left to try to convince you. It's only fair that you give me a chance."

She nodded. "Of course," she murmured.

"Our business relationship is very successful," he continued earnestly. "Our marriage could be an extension of that. A partnership. A business arrangement. We won't expect anything more from each other." He covered her hand with his. "You said it yourself. We're not in love with each other."

She stared into his eyes, wondering if he really didn't see that she was falling for him. The more she saw of him, the more she saw to love. When she'd said they weren't in love with each other, she'd been using it as a defense, trying to keep him from stealing her heart away. But she knew now that she'd been trying to bar the door after the horse had already left the stable. Did he really not sense the way her emotions were building? Or didn't he care?

"Don't you see that not being in love gives us a lot of freedom?" he went on, warming to his theory. "I think where people go wrong is when they expect too much from each other. When they are unrealistic.

Expectations get too high and neither can meet them. If we map this out ahead of time and know exactly what we're each bringing to this union, exactly where we think we're going, how can we go wrong?''

"How, indeed," she murmured, wincing.

He moved closer so that he could speak to her in a very low voice.

"Maggie, this is very emotional for me. More emotional than I ever would have thought it could be." His eyes darkened and his voice dropped even lower. "You see, I never thought I would have children. I never planned to marry again."

She nodded, biting her lip. She knew his first marriage had been a disaster, but she didn't know the details.

"When I was told that I had a child out there somewhere, it hit me like…like lightning going right through me. I never dreamed I would care so much. I was overwhelmed. And then to find out that you are the one…"

To her surprise, his voice choked, and he looked away.

"Well, it just seems so perfect," he went on huskily. "I mean, I really like you. And I respect you." His gaze met hers again. "And your child needs a father. And I guess I'm the guy."

That did it. Now she had a lump in her throat. She coughed, hoping to dislodge it, but it stayed right where it was. There was no way she could say anything without starting to cry. And then she would feel exactly like a fool. So she stayed mum.

"I'm not asking for a whole lot," he went on. "In fact, it's more that I want to give you something than that I want to take anything from you."

She looked into his eyes. He was right. She was acting as though she had to keep him at bay, as if she thought he was trying to rob her of her child. And from his point of view, what he was offering was protection, security and a father for a child she'd expected to raise without one. How could she turn down all this goodness?

And yet…and yet…

She saw Tom's face again, heard the ugly words that cut into her like shards of broken glass, remembered how miserable she'd been, remembered how what at first seemed good could turn so bad. Could she risk living like that again?

Kane wasn't Tom. She'd told herself that again and again, and she believed it. And yet…

She wasn't ready to make that commitment, but she didn't know how to explain it to him. Thinking quickly, she grasped at another problem she saw in his plan.

"Kane, I appreciate your honesty. I really do. And I understand your idea of a business partnership. I'm just not sure it can work."

His brows drew together. "Why not?"

She hesitated. "You say it will be a purely business arrangement. That means, I assume, it will be platonic. But…'' She licked her bottom lip nervously and avoided his gaze. ''This is embarrassing, but…it seems to me that we have a bit of a physical attraction. Maybe you don't feel it…'' she added hastily, looking up into his face.

But he was laughing softly and he took her hand. ''Oh, you noticed?'' he said, smiling at her. ''Believe me, Maggie. I feel it.''

That was a relief. And a danger. She didn't know which was more important.

''Maggie, I don't think you should worry about that,'' he was saying, shrugging her fears away. ''I know women always take that sort of thing much more seriously than men do. But men can control themselves too. We're human beings, Maggie, not beasts of the jungle being pulled this way and that by primal impulses we don't understand. We can handle it.''

Could they? Why did she have this little ache inside that said the opposite? But maybe *he* didn't. Maybe he thought the chemistry between them was just one of those things—no big deal. Perhaps he felt this way with most attractive women he met. And how about her? How did she feel? She only wished she knew.

''So you think we're very modern, do you?'' she asked him brightly.

''Sure.''

Her smile was bittersweet. ''I think you're dreaming.''

"Why, Maggie." He gave her a quizzical look, meant for teasing. "Are you trying to tell me you don't think you're going to be able to keep your hands off me?"

"Dream on, mister," she told him tartly, though she knew her cheeks were coloring. "I'll challenge you to a self-control contest any day."

His eyes lit with amusement at that. "I just might take you up on that," he told her, bringing her hand to his lips and kissing her fingers, though his gaze never left her face. "In the meantime, what do you say? Will you marry me?"

"Oh, Kane..."

"It might just work if we can keep it on a business level and not let things get too personal."

"Do you really think that's possible?" She shook her head. "I just don't see how it could work."

"Why wouldn't it?" His gaze intensified. "Maggie, we both married for love the first time. Now we'll marry for more practical reasons. You wait and see. Things will work out much better this way."

She searched his eyes. She wished she could believe the way he did. She wanted to say the words he wanted to hear, but she couldn't. Too much of her life had taught her that optimism was a way of asking fate to cut your legs out from under you.

And at the same time, she cared about him, cared too much. She couldn't give him the words he wanted, but she wanted to give him something, and she reached out with her hand and put her palm to his cheek.

"Kane..." she began softly.

He covered her hand with his own and his eyes glowed. For just a moment, she was sure he was going to kiss her. But a woman's voice cut them apart like a knife slicing through ripe fruit.

"Kane Haley! You old rascal."

Jerking away from each other, they turned to see a beautiful woman with a model's face and a playgirl's figure standing behind Kane's chair. Kane rose reluctantly and the woman gave him the full flirt treatment, batting eyelashes and everything.

"You naughty boy, you were supposed to call me before the Zimmerman Charity Ball." Her gorgeous wide mouth twisted in a little-girl pout. "Where have you been?"

"Jasparina," he said with casual unconcern. "Sorry. I've been busy. Please meet Maggie Steward...my fiancée."

The woman looked the tiniest bit taken aback, but her smooth sophistication took over immediately and she smiled her plastic smile and shook Maggie's hand. "Congratulations, darling," she purred, though it was not easy to tell which one she was talking to. "I'm with a party across the room. Why don't you join us? Kane, some of your old friends are there...."

"Sorry. We're newly engaged and in a hurry to grab a little time for ourselves," he told her. "We were just leaving.'' And he reached for Maggie's hand to help her to her feet.

Maggie rose and looked from one to the other of these beautiful people. Kane was dismissing Jasparina out of hand. She could see it, and so could the raven-haired beauty. And Maggie knew why without having to analyze it.

The beauty wasn't carrying his baby. But Maggie was. And right now, that was all that mattered to him.

But to introduce her as his fiancée! She cast him an outraged look and gave Jasparina a stiff little smile before heading for the door.

As they made their way to where the valet-parking attendant was holding their car, she found herself laughing with Kane about the incident.

''What are you doing?'' she cried, turning her coat collar against a stiff wind off the lake.

''Forcing the issue,'' he told her with a grin as he pulled her into the circle of his arm. He looked down into her face. ''Maggie I can feel you trembling on the verge of saying yes. Come on. Do it.''

''Kane...'' She was losing her resolve. It was melting away like the snow along the sidewalk.

''Do it!''

''Oh...'' She was caught up in his wonderful smile. ''Yes!''

''Yes,'' he echoed, but his voice was reverential, and he pulled her close and kissed her hard on the mouth.

* * *

Maggie and Kane were getting married. She had a hard time focusing on the reality of her situation. Joy and fear kept tumbling after one another in her heart.

She was marrying the boss. What a cliché. She was having the boss's baby. In another age, that would have been an insurmountable scandal. Now it was mostly harmless fodder for the gossip mill. But what would they all say once they knew? It made her blush to think.

The first people who had to know were Kane's brother and sister-in-law, and they planned to have dinner with them almost right away. Maggie was nervous about it. What were these people who loved Kane going to think about him marrying his administrative assistant whom he had never given a second thought to before? What were they going to say about this crazy arrangement?

Kane drove them to Mark and Jill's house and Maggie looked out the window as they cruised through a neighborhood very much like the one she'd grown up in. The houses were neat and two-story with wide front yards currently covered with snow. She had a sudden memory of the smell of apple pie baking, the sound of the radio playing her mother's favorite classical music and the boys next door wearing their lettermen's jackets and yelling good-naturedly to each other as they came home from a hockey game. That was life in the neighborhoods. For some reason, tears came to her eyes as she thought of it. She'd lived in apartments too long.

Mark's house was one of the nicest on his block, with a huge yard and trees in small clumps making it look as though the home were in the middle of a forest glen. As they went into the house, she could feel the warmth of the family that lived there even before she saw one of them.

Two little redheads came barreling down the stairs, leaping in the air with cries of triumph to land on their uncle. Kane caught them both and threw them down on the couch, tickling and wrestling and generally making them shriek with delight. Then he brought them both upright and introduced them to Maggie.

"Kenny and Jennifer," he told her. "Say hello to your new aunt, kids."

"Hi," Jennifer said stoutly. A pretty little girl of about six, she was bright-eyed and friendly.

Kenny was younger and shyer, looking down at his pajama-covered feet and grunting his greeting.

"He'll talk to you later," Jennifer told her confidentially. "He has to get to know you first."

"I'll be looking forward to it," Maggie said with a smile.

There were various greetings as Jill and Mark entered the room, and then Jill was herding the children up to bed and Mark was showing Maggie his rare book collection. All things considered, they were making her feel very much at home.

Jill had made a mouthwatering cioppino and warmed sourdough rolls to go with it. She served the wonderful seafood stew in wide-lipped soup bowls and gave a running commentary about her Italian background as she spooned it out.

"How unusual," Maggie noted, "for an Italian to have such red hair."

Mark gave a quick burst of laughter. "Not really," he said. "See, she forgot to tell you that her mother is Irish. For some reason, she keeps leaving that out of the picture."

"I do not," Jill retorted. "I just hadn't gotten to it yet."

They all laughed, and Jill proceeded to recount how her Irish grandparents had arrived in New York without a penny to their name and ended up owning and operating a bed-and-breakfast on Cape Cod.

"We never had much money in my family, but we spent every vacation in one of the best spots in the country."

Maggie watched the interplay between Mark and Jill. It was obvious from the moment you saw them together that they were a team and that they loved each other very much. How did that happen? Was it just blind luck? Was it careful planning? Or did it take a certain personality to be able to mold your life with another's?

Whatever it was, she envied it—and wished she knew the secret.

At the same time, she found herself watching Kane

and seeing him with new eyes. This was a side of him she hadn't known before. He was laughing and talking with his brother in a way that showed a deep affection between them and teasing his sister-in-law in a way that showed a wary regard that was loving, but just a little prickly around the edges. No doubt about it, Kane was a first-class guy. What would their relationship look like in another year? Would people be able to tell how they related to each other just by looking at them? Only time would tell.

Both of Kane's relatives seemed to be very happy about his plans to marry Maggie. The only thing that gave them pause was the claim that their marriage would be for convenience only.

"You understand, this is entirely a business arrangement," Kane told them earnestly as he finished the last of his roll. "We're making a bargain here. We're not marrying for love."

"Yes, so I understand." Jill looked sideways at Maggie for confirmation.

"No, not at all," she said firmly, hoping she was making a convincing case.

"You see, we don't love each other," Kane told them with a shrug, speaking as though it were the most natural thing in the world. "We are marrying as the best way to take care of our child. End of issue."

"Uh-huh." Jill's eyes narrowed thoughtfully as she looked from one to the other of them. "I understand completely."

Maggie sensed the cynicism in her tone, and she reacted defensively. "No, really, it's true. I've been married before and so has he. We both know the score.'' She didn't think Jill was buying it, and she went on, trying harder and harder to convince her. ''I mean, if you just look at this objectively, you can see that I'm not Kane's type at all. We would never have gotten together if it weren't for the baby.''

Kane frowned, not sure he was crazy about the turn the conversation was taking.

''What do you think Kane's type is?'' Jill asked curiously.

But Maggie was on solid ground here. ''Are you kidding? I used to arrange his dates for him.'' Maggie sent Kane a challenging smile. ''I've sent so many bouquets as morning-after flowers....''

''Not lately,'' Kane said defensively.

''True. Not lately.''

''I've been too busy to date over the last year or so. Remember the TriPac merger? We worked night and day on that. And then there was this whole search for my baby.''

''Of course.'' It surprised her that he seemed this displeased with the issue. After all, his well-known playboy past only made a stronger case for the basis of their marriage. Anyone with any sense knew she was not the sort of woman Kane Haley usually had on his arm as he cruised the town.

But now, she would be. That thought made her gasp softly. Was it really true? How could this be happening? One part of her was thrilled—and the other part was saying, ''Just wait. Your happiness won't last.''

"We're not going to have any sort of ceremony," Kane was explaining. "We'll just go to City Hall on Friday and have it done."

"Ah," said Jill. "Like a tetanus shot."

Kane threw her a scowl and went on as though she hadn't spoken. "We would like to have the two of you as witnesses. If you have the time, I mean. If you're not busy that day."

"Of course," Mark said cheerfully. "We'll be there with bells on."

"And maybe some clothes, besides," Jill murmured.

"It should be short and sweet," Kane told them. "We'll just do the paperwork, say the vows and go to lunch or something." He looked at Maggie for confirmation. "Then get back to work."

"Really? That simple?" Jill gave Mark a significant look and kicked him under the table. "How very post-modern of you."

Mark looked worried, as though he knew his wife was up to something, but Jill leaned forward and said, "Let us take you to lunch after the marriage thingee at City Hall. Okay? Let me make the plans."

"Sure," Kane said, raising a questioning eyebrow at Maggie, who smiled in agreement. "That would be very nice."

They finished dinner, and Mark took Maggie aside to show her an old photo album with pictures of Kane as a youngster. Maggie crowed over them. Kane was definitely a charmer as a toddler. Then Kane and

Mark went out to rent a movie while Jill and Maggie cleaned up the dishes. Jill got right to the point.

"Well, you're probably curious about Kane's first wife and first marriage."

Maggie almost dropped a dish. "Oh. Well, yes, but…"

"Yes, I know." Jill started rinsing off dishes and handing them to Maggie to put in the dishwasher. "You should ask Kane about it and let him tell you himself. But we both know he won't tell you."

Maggie hid a grin. "That's probably true."

"We know it's true. But I think you have a right to know. In fact, you absolutely should know." She handed her the last dish, switched off the water and turned to lean with her back against the sink. "You shouldn't jump into things like this without knowing the track record."

Maggie nodded. "You're right."

"So here goes." She crossed her arms over her chest. "Crystal was tall, she was elegant, she was beautiful. I couldn't stand her. She was what they call an 'expensive woman.' Very high-maintenance."

"Oh." Maggie put the last dish into the washer and rose, turning to look at the pictures held by magnets on Jill's refrigerator. Anything to keep from letting Jill see how this was affecting her.

"What, you may ask, did Kane see in her?" Jill went on. "Well, we know love is blind. And I guess he really did think he loved her." She sighed. "That's what makes it so great that the two of you aren't in love with each other. You're both going into this with eyes wide open.''

Maggie turned quickly to look into Jill's eyes. She was joking, wasn't she? But no. Her gaze was completely guileless.

"Yes," Maggie said a bit breathlessly.

"Well, to continue, about Kane and Crystal. Kane could afford an expensive woman. But Kane is a very smart man. And once the first glow of intoxication died away, he began to notice that she seemed to love money a lot more than she loved anything human. So he wasn't quite so generous with it any longer. And the less he gave, the more she raved, and finally, she cashed in her chips and went looking for a new sugar daddy.''

"You mean...she only married him for his money?" What an appalling thought. How could anyone marry Kane and not love him? She knew she wasn't going to be able to do it. But she couldn't tell Jill that. On the other hand, she had a sneaking suspicion Jill might just know. She looked at her more closely.

Jill could make a killing playing poker, she thought to herself.

"They didn't like each other at all by the end," Jill was saying. "She told me to my face that she only had so many years being this beautiful, and she thought she deserved to get more for it. That was how much she valued her marriage vows.''

"Oh, that's awful. Poor Kane."

"You have to admit, there was a certain logic to that. After all, once she isn't beautiful any more she'll be out in the cold. She certainly doesn't have any personality traits to compensate." Jill made a face. "Anyway, Kane doesn't often make the same mistake twice. I think he had an inkling of what she was like, but he thought marriage would change her. Kind of a twist on the old saw that women think they can change the men they marry." Jill shook her head. "People can't be transformed so easily. It has to come from within them if anything real is going to change. And if it doesn't happen, it doesn't happen. And in this case, it didn't happen."

Did he still have any feelings for Crystal, Maggie wondered? Had his bad marriage made him as gun-shy as hers had made her? Apparently not. He was the one pushing for the marriage, after all.

"If Kane and I have any problems I can promise you it won't be along those lines," she said.

"Oh no. I knew that." Jill smiled at her. "As a matter of fact, I think you're perfect for Kane."

Maggie had to laugh at her matter-of-fact statement. "Why do you say that? You barely know me."

Jill didn't elaborate. "You know, Kane really never was the marrying type," she went on instead. "He dated like crazy when he was young, a different girl every night. He never got serious about anyone until Crystal. Something about her seemed to speak to him in a strange way."

She hesitated, as though not sure if she should be saying this much. Moving closer, she touched Maggie's arm and spoke softly. "My theory is that she came from an old Boston family, just like his father did. And that was what intrigued him."

"His father?" Maggie gazed at her blankly. "I thought he died when Kane was very young."

"He did. But it had a major effect on Kane's life." Jill drew back, grabbed a sponge and began wiping down the counter. "I think that story is one Kane ought to tell you about, not me."

Maggie didn't push her. She'd already heard a lot of new information she was going to need time to digest. She went back to looking at the pictures, finding one of Kane throwing a snowball at the camera, but mostly they were of the two children. When she looked back, she found Jill dishing up cherry cobbler, and she turned to get the vanilla ice cream out of the freezer. They chatted while fixing their dessert plates, then carried them out to the table to await the return of the men.

"It's too bad," Jill said as they wandered out into the living room and dropped onto the couch. "There's so little time to do a proper wedding. You won't have time to get the gown treatment and the whole bit. But, of course, you had that in your first wedding, didn't you?"

"Actually, no," Maggie admitted. "We sort of eloped."

"No gown?" Jill said, her face stricken. "Not ever?"

"No." Maggie smiled. "Don't worry about it. I can cope."

Jill looked skeptical. "I take it that you're still mourning your first husband to a certain extent," she commented.

"No." Maggie thought she might as well get it out in the open.

"No?" Jill looked as though she thought she hadn't heard right. "What do you mean, no?"

"No, I'm not mourning him. Where did you get that idea?"

Jill frowned. "Kane told me. At least, that was my impression."

Maggie shook her head. "I never told him that. I don't know why he thinks it."

"Because it would seem natural, I guess. But you say no."

Maggie turned and looked into Jill's gaze. "Jill, my first marriage was not particularly happy. While it was sad that Tom died at such a young age, in some ways, it was something of a relief for me. I was miserable being married to him."

Jill reached out and took her hand. "Oh, Maggie, I'm so sorry. I had no idea."

"That is one reason why I've been so hesitant about marrying again," she said, then regretted it. After all, Jill didn't know anything about that.

But Jill didn't even seem to notice. "I don't think

Kane knows about this,'' she was saying instead.
''Perhaps you'd better tell him.''

Of course she should tell him. But there never
seemed to be any time.

Kane Knows about Maggie's new suit during married Believes with name will and Of course, she should get her.. plus their news seemed to be anymore.

Chapter Seven

Married! Maggie was getting married. Was it time to panic?

No. She couldn't afford to panic. She was doing this for her baby, and she was going to do it right. She dressed carefully, wearing a new silk suit that was a little snug in the waist. And then she waited, staring at the second hand as it made its way around the face of the clock.

Kane came to get her at ten.

"Are you nervous?" he asked, passing his gloves from one hand to the other and back again.

"No," she responded. "I'm petrified."

"Join the crowd," he muttered under his breath as he picked up her overnight case and looked around. "Anything else?" he said.

She shook her head. It seemed strange to think she

wouldn't be coming back that night. Just before closing the door, she looked back and thought, Goodbye, Tom. Goodbye old life. And then she turned away while Kane shut the door.

They didn't say much on the drive to City Hall. Mark and Jill were waiting for them at the entrance, and they went in together. There were papers to sign and finally a bored-looking official had them raise their hands and swear, and, suddenly, they were married.

Maggie looked down at the ring Kane slipped on her finger, then up into his eyes. She saw herself in their flat reflection. This didn't feel right. There should be more to it.

"Let's go," Jill said perkily. "We've got reservations at the club."

She was talking about the country club where Mark and Kane both played golf. Jill was more into tennis, as she told them at length as they walked back to the cars. Funny, but she was the only one who said anything at all, until Kane said, "We'll follow you," nodding toward where he'd parked.

And then they were alone again in the car. Maggie was beginning to get a headache and the baby was squirming. Kane wasn't talking. Did he feel as creepy about this as she did? But she had no right to feel that way. This was something good they were doing. If she'd wanted something more than the City Hall utilitarianism she should have told Kane so. He would have done whatever she wanted and she knew it. She had no right to complain after the fact. This was her own darn fault. But to tell the truth, she wanted to cry.

The parking lot at the country club was full.

"Do people play golf in the snow?" she asked, frowning at all the cars as she tried to stabilize her emotions.

"No," Kane said shortly. "There's probably a banquet or something."

She got out of the car and started toward the entrance to the long, low building, but Jill caught up with her and pulled her to the side.

"Come in this way," she said. "Through the ladies' locker room. I've got something to show you."

She followed Jill, feeling numb, and then she was blinking in the dim light of the locker room. After the bright sunshine, she was partly blinded, but it seemed to her that there was a dress looming in the gloom. As her eyes adjusted, it got clearer.

Sure enough, there before her on a mannequin was the most beautiful wedding gown she'd ever seen. Antique white satin and chiffon made in an A-line style with an Empire waist, the bodice shimmered with bead work and embroidery while the skirt extended into a beaded train and the lacy sleeves fell to wrist length.

"Oooh," she said, and all her disappointment with the day was plain in the longing of her tone.

"Do you like it?" Jill asked with an impish grin.

"Of course." Maggie turned and frowned at Jill.

"Well, start stripping, honey. You're going to put it on."

"What?" She couldn't have heard right.

"I can only hope that it fits," Jill said crisply. "That Empire waist should help. But I've got a seamstress on call in case we need her. Hurry up! They're waiting to see the bride."

"Jill…" She wanted to ask who was waiting, but things were moving too fast and she didn't get the question out in time. The next thing she knew she was sliding into the lovely gown, and it fitted fine. Turning to look at herself in the full-length mirror, she was stunned by what she saw. How could one pretty dress make such a transformation?

"Oh!" she said, "Oh, Jill!"

"Here," Jill said. "Let me tidy up your hair. Don't need to do much, because the veil will cover it all."

"But Jill…"

"Hurry! No time for questions. Let's go."

Jill hustled her toward the main banquet room. Funny, there seemed to be organ music playing. It sounded an awful lot like the traditional wedding march. But before Maggie could think through what that might mean, Jill pulled her right into the room and she was too startled by what she saw to wonder about it anymore.

The room was crowded with people, and they were all people she recognized. Just about everyone who worked at Kane Haley, Inc., seemed to be present. As she gazed about, mouth open in surprise, the crowd parted and she saw Kane, looking incredibly handsome in a tuxedo, waiting at the other side of the room with Mark beside him and someone who looked very much like a minister.

"Jill!" she cried, but Jill was shooing her two children, Jennifer and Kenny, dressed up and wearing patent-leather shoes, on down the aisle before them. Jennifer carried a basket of rose petals and the two of them were strewing the petals along the path—though Kenny did seem prone to dropping them in clumps instead of floating them at random as his sister did.

"You get going, too," Jill whispered to Maggie as the music swelled, thrusting a bouquet of violets into her hands. "I'll be right behind you."

Maggie didn't really have to ask what was going on any longer. It was pretty obvious. Shaking her head in wonder, she turned and started down the aisle behind the children; she could feel herself begin to radiate happiness. And there was Kane smiling at her, his eyes shining with admiration for how she looked. She smiled back, hoping he could see how great she thought he looked. And suddenly it seemed as if magic was happening. The music, the flowers, the smiling onlookers—now *this* was what she would call a wedding!

She hardly heard the service being given by the minister. A warm, happy glow seemed to encase her and everyone around her. She managed to say "I do" at the right time, but she must have said it a little too eagerly, because there were those among the onlookers who laughed. And when the words "You may kiss the bride," were heard, she turned to Kane and welcomed him with all her heart.

Everyone applauded and Maggie and Kane turned to smile at them and wave. Then they led the way, prompted by Jill, into the next banquet room which was set up with food on long tables. Maggie held Kane's hand very tightly.

"Were you in on this?" she whispered to him as they walked, smiling at their friends in the crowd.

"Not really. Jill did ask me to let everyone at Kane Haley off for the day, to celebrate our wedding, so I knew something was up." He shook his head. "That's Jill. Think you can take a life with her always lurking in the background, ready to make everything better for you?"

Maggie laughed. Right now, she considered her sister-in-law her very best friend ever. They took their places at the head of the receiving line and Jill popped in next to Maggie as they began shaking hands and accepting congratulations.

"You!" Maggie gave her a hug. "Why did you do this? *How* did you do it? You had so little time!"

"They don't call me the pint-sized steamroller for nothing. Besides, I had help," she added, gesturing toward where CeCe stood watching them.

Maggie smiled and CeCe waved, mouthing, "Don't blame me!" as usual.

Jill linked arms with her new sister-in-law. "I'm so glad you're happy about it. Once I got the ball rolling, I thought 'Oh no! What if she really didn't want a real wedding for some reason? What if she hates religion? What if she's allergic to wedding cake?' But I soon got over it and went ahead."

"I'm glad you did. I was so depressed at City Hall…."

"I could tell." Jill smiled at her. "But I promise not to spring too many things on you in the future. This was the first and the last."

And probably the best. Maggie was ecstatic. Someone got her a plate of food, but she was too excited to eat, and she was too busy going from one group of people to another, thanking them for coming and accepting their congratulations. She wasn't used to being the focus of so much attention, and she had to admit, she really liked it.

But every few minutes she turned to find where Kane was. And as likely as not, though all the way across the wide room, he was turning to find her at the same time. Their eyes would meet and they would smile and it seemed as though a secret message passed between them every time.

Then Maggie would go back to talking to friends and coworkers. She was particularly glad to have a chance to chat with her best friends from the office, Julia Oman, Sharon Waterton, Lauren Mitchell and Jen Holder. All had been married very recently, giving them a lot in common.

"So, I just heard you're having Kane's baby!" Julia exclaimed, shaking back her sleek dark-blond hair and looking happily pregnant herself.

"I'm having *our* baby."

"Oh, of course." Julia gave her a hug. "I'm sorry. We're all just so surprised."

"I can't tell you how happy everyone is about this," Sharon chimed in, her hand on her own very prominently pregnant tummy. "Everyone thinks you're terrific. And of course, we all adore Kane. Most of the time," she added with a laugh.

"He can be difficult at times, can't he?" Maggie agreed with obvious affection.

"He's a man!" Lauren said, "What can I tell you?"

They all laughed along with her, and then had to examine what they could see of Maggie's stomach.

"So, will you be working after the baby is old enough?" Jen asked. She herself had recently returned to her work as Benefits Manager since delivering a beautiful baby in November.

"We really haven't discussed it, but I'm hoping to come in at least a few days a week. After all, we've got our wonderful new day-care center. That will make it so much easier."

"The day-care center." Julia exchanged glances with the others. "Uh-huh. Listen, uh…"

Maggie looked at her questioningly. "What's the matter?"

"Oh nothing," Lauren said quickly. "This isn't the time."

"Tell me. Or I'll be worrying all night."

"Well, we certainly wouldn't want you to be distracted." They all laughed at Jen's smart-aleck remark, though Maggie felt just a little embarrassed. How could she ever explain to these women that this marriage was not going to include a lot of lovemaking on the honeymoon? Never mind. Let them think whatever they wanted to.

"No, now, tell me about the day-care center. Is something wrong?"

"Okay," Julia said at last. "It's just that…well, there are rumors running rampant that it's not going to happen."

"What?"

"You hadn't heard?"

"No!" But a part of her remembered that Kane had reacted strangely when last she'd brought it up.

"Don't let it bother you," Lauren said quickly. "Not on a day like this. We can talk about it when you get back to work."

"Well, that will be tomorrow."

"Really? What about your honeymoon?"

"Oh, we're not going anywhere."

"You aren't?" Julia looked surprised. "Then what did we take up that collection for?"

Maggie looked at her blankly. "I don't know what you're talking about."

"Oh, now I've ruined the surprise," Julia wailed.

"A bunch of us chipped in and got you three nights at the Chivas Ritz. Starting tonight, of course."

"Oh no!"

Luckily, Maggie's stricken look didn't seem to register with the others. They chattered on about what a wonderful hotel it was, and how they hoped Maggie and Kane would have a wonderful time. In the meantime Maggie was trying to keep a smile on her face while thinking desperately of how she could get out of this.

A honeymoon! No, that hadn't been in the plan. She wasn't sure why staying in a hotel for a honeymoon was so much more dangerous than her moving into the penthouse apartment with Kane, but it was. It just was.

They cut the cake, and Maggie tossed her bouquet and they were officially presented with the honeymoon present from the employees. People began to drift away and she and Kane went to the respective locker rooms, changed back into their street clothes, and headed for their car amid cheers from the remaining celebrants.

"Can you believe this?" Maggie said to Kane as they made their way onto the highway. "All these people….they've been so nice to us…it makes me want to cry."

Funny. She'd wanted to cry for a completely different reason when they'd arrived. Now she was *really* married. She sneaked a look at Kane and suddenly her heart was in her throat. Really married.

The room was spectacular. It sported a round bed, two bathrooms, a Jacuzzi bath and a wide view of the Chicago skyline and the lake. A huge fruit basket sat waiting, along with a box of expensive chocolates and a bottle of champagne and two flutes. Everything a normal newly wed couple would need for a perfect honeymoon. Only, they weren't normal.

And that made things awkward. They both unpacked and changed into something more casual and then turned around and looked at each other a little nervously.

"Let's go for a walk," Kane said impulsively.

"It's thirty-eight degrees out."

"We'll dress warmly." He reached out a hand toward her. "Come on. Let's walk out on the Navy Pier."

She put her hand in his. "All right," she said, meeting his gaze.

He smiled. She was going to trust him. That was a good thing. "Let's go."

The walkway around the Navy Pier was deserted, though music was playing through the sound system all along the way. They walked quickly, huddling together every time a frigid gust off the lake slapped at them, laughing most of the time. When they had finally had enough of the cold they went inside the building and used the inner walkway. Here was where the people were, along with tourist vendors and food carts. Kane bought a hot dog and tried to get her to share, but she claimed she was still too excited to eat anything. They sat on a wooden bench and watched a clown entertaining a group of preschool children.

"In just a few years our little one will be in pre-school," Maggie mused.

"Don't rush things," he told her, licking mustard from his finger. "Let's enjoy the babyhood first."

She looked at him curiously. "Why did you think you'd never have children?" she asked him.

"Are you serious? All you have to do is look at them." He waved a hand in the direction of the pre-schoolers. "They're noisy and grubby and annoying. They whine, they cry, they demand dessert and beg for toys." He shrugged, feeling as though he'd pretty much made his case. "They're nothing but trouble."

She gaped at him in astonishment. "You don't like kids?" she demanded.

"That was a little louder than it needed to be," he told her out of the corner of his mouth as a few of the smaller children turned to gape at the man who didn't like them. "But the fact is, no, I'm not a kid person at all."

She twisted her mouth, thinking. "You don't seem to feel that way about your niece and nephew," she noted.

"Oh." He had to admit she had a point there. But there was a logical explanation. "Well, that's different. *They're* great kids."

"Uh-huh." A grin was beginning to spread to her eyes. "So the only children you actually know, you adore."

"Well…" He gave her a slightly exasperated look. "I guess you could say that."

She laughed and casually linked her arm with his in a way she'd never done voluntarily before. He noticed, and he liked it. In fact, he liked her. Liked her a whole lot. And that was something he was going to have to keep a leash on.

They took a cab back to the hotel. Kane flopped on the bed and Maggie sank into a big chair and they turned on music. Kane seemed to be sleeping so Maggie didn't bother him. But she couldn't help but enjoy the way he looked stretched out on the bed. She'd never seen him in that position before. It was difficult to keep from imagining what it would feel like to slide in beside him.

"We have two decisions to make," she told him after a lazy half hour had passed and she saw him stirring.

"Hmmm?" he responded drowsily.

"Number one, what will we do about dinner? And number two, what will we do about that bed?"

He opened one eye and looked at her. "You think it might look odd if we called down and had the bell-boy bring up a roll-away?"

She thought about it for a moment. That would be the most logical thing to do. But somehow she couldn't feature doing it. She could just imagine the gossip racing like a brush fire through the hotel staff. "The honeymoon couple called down for a roll-away!" She cringed. No, she couldn't face that.

She looked at Kane. He grinned as though he'd read her mind.

"Don't worry," he told her, rolling over to sit on the side of the bed. "We'll work something out before bedtime. And as for dinner, Jill has that covered, too. All we have to do is call down and tell them we're ready. They'll bring a special feast, ordered up by my incredibly energetic and know-it-all sister-in-law, right up here to the room."

The dinner was delicious. Maggie wondered if Jill had an ulterior motive for keeping them in the room together instead of out among others in a restaurant, but she didn't discuss her suspicions with Kane, and they chatted about inconsequential things while they ate, then watched a little TV, and then it was time to go to sleep.

"You take the bed," Kane told her firmly. "You're the one who's pregnant. I can rig something up here with the chair and a couple of ottomans."

She felt a bit guilty letting him take the uncomfortable setup, but there didn't seem to be any choice in the matter. She went into the bathroom and put on her nightgown and robe, then came out feeling very self-conscious, only to find Kane engrossed in a book.

"Good night," she said, looking over as she dropped the robe and slid under the covers.

"'Night," he mumbled, and didn't even look up from his reading.

She felt relief and chagrin all at the same time. But

not for long, because within a couple of minutes, she was sound asleep.

Kane finally looked over once he heard her even breathing. Letting the book fall from his hand, he watched her for a long, long time, taking in the swirl of her blond hair, the curve of her cheek, her dark lashes against her creamy skin. A smile teased his lips, and he shook his head, got up and headed for the bathroom to make his own preparations for sleep. He was a married man again.

"Let's hope there's a happy ending this time," he murmured to himself as he left the room.

Chapter Eight

Maggie woke up the next morning to find herself alone. Kane had left a note telling her he'd gone on down to breakfast and to meet him in the coffee shop. She smiled to herself as she read it. Surely he was being tactful, allowing her to get up and get dressed on this first morning of their marriage without the embarrassment of having him underfoot. She appreciated his sensitivity and hurried to prepare to meet him.

When she walked into the restaurant, he looked up and smiled, and she smiled back and the day was off to a great start.

"What are we going to do with all this time off?" she asked rather pathetically over orange juice. It was strange, but she sort of missed having the structure of a job to go to.

Kane put his head to the side, thinking, then snapped his fingers and nodded. "We'll do the city," he said. "We'll pretend we've never been to Chicago before and we'll do the tourist thing."

And they did, starting off with a trip up to the ninety-sixth floor of the John Hancock Building to look at the spectacular view. The rest of the day was spent sashaying through the parks and museums as though they'd never seen them before—and in some cases, they hadn't. They talked and laughed and teased each other, and Maggie realized she was having a day like no other. Being with Kane was like being with a best friend and a handsome lover all at once. The only trouble was, he wasn't really a lover. And she wanted to make sure things stayed that way, despite the fact that each touch, even just to steady her with a hand on her elbow, made her heartbeat race and her breath seem short.

That evening they ate at a wonderful Italian restaurant on Grand Avenue and afterwards Kane took her to one of his favorite jazz clubs where they listened to cool jazz and sipped fruit juice instead of martinis. They took a horse-drawn carriage back to the hotel and went right to bed.

"Why don't you take the bed tonight?" Maggie offered. She'd noticed his back had been a little stiff that morning. "We should take turns."

"Get in bed," he ordered, flipping back the covers for her. "There's no way I'm letting you sleep anywhere else. After all, you've got my baby with you. He needs to get a good night's sleep."

"Oh!" she said, putting a hand on her gently rounded stomach, and suddenly she was very ready to get into the bed. "Speaking of your son," she said, gritting her teeth. "He seems to be complaining about all the walking we've been doing the last two days. Ouch! Hey, kid. Have some respect for your elders!"

Kane stood over the bed looking uncharacteristically unsure of himself. He watched as she rubbed where the baby had kicked. Looking up, she thought she knew what he was thinking.

She reached for his hand and drew it down. "Right here," she told him, pressing his palm down over the spot. "You have to keep quiet and wait. You'll feel a sort of flutter."

The baby moved again, and Kane's face changed.

"Was that it?" he said, his eyes luminous. "I think I felt…ohmigod, that's him."

He was transfixed. Dropping down to sit beside where she lay, he put both hands on her stomach, moving slightly, searching for more evidence of the baby.

She had to grin. She'd only been feeling all this movement fairly recently, and she remembered when she'd first felt something she was sure was the real thing. The thrill had been unlike anything she'd ever experienced. A real life was growing inside her! She knew he was feeling something close to that himself, and she felt the joy again as though it were the first time. There was no doubt about it, sharing this experience was so much better than living it alone.

"They say it gets much wilder by the seventh month or so," she told him. "Sometimes you can actually see little elbows and feet pushing out."

He grinned. "That is so…" He couldn't seem to find a word to express just how great this was, and his voice died away as he felt her stomach again, his eyes full of wonder. Sitting back, he smiled at her.

"I'll be honest with you, Maggie. As I've told you before, I never in a thousand years would have thought I would get this emotional about this baby stuff. If someone had told me a few months ago that I would soon be running around like a crazy person searching for my child, and then, having found my child, be contemplating marriage, I would have laughed in their face. I would have said they were nuts."

She smiled at him. "And they would have been nuts. Because that wasn't you then."

"No, it wasn't me then." He put his head to the side, considering. "I'm a different person."

"I know. I'm a different person, too. Becoming a parent really changes you."

He looked down at her, all curiosity, and took her hand in his. "How?" he asked.

Suddenly he wanted to know, wanted to be a part of whatever that change was. He wanted to experience this as fully as he could.

She tried to think of how to explain to him. "It's

almost as though I entered a different layer of existence. I'm aware of things I never noticed before.''

"Sure," he said. He knew just what she meant. "Exactly."

"Of course," she went on, ever full of common sense, "everything new you do can create that feeling in you. When you learn a new skill or try art work or learn to tap dance. Or…or fall in love…."

Their gazes met and both quickly darted away. Somehow it was embarrassing that they weren't in love with each other. He reached out and put his hand on her stomach again, waiting for a sensation that didn't come this time.

"I think he's gone to sleep," he said, disappointed.

Their gazes met again and suddenly they both realized, now that the baby had stopped moving, she was lying there in her sheer nightgown and he was leaning over her with both hands on her body.

He swallowed and began to inch away. She bit her lip and reached for the covers. In another moment, he was up and talking about something they'd seen that day, and she was turning on her side and trying to pretend her heart wasn't racing in her chest.

He puttered about the room and then got into the pajama bottoms he wore to sleep in. Maggie didn't fall asleep this time, and she saw him as he came out of the bathroom, the lamplight casting a golden glow on his bare and beautifully muscled chest, the pajama bottom slung low on his tight hips. She had to fight back the gasp that threatened to come up her throat and turn her face into the pillow. Oh, why did he have to be so darn gorgeous?

He turned off the light and got into his chair-bed. They both lay still with their eyes wide open. Somehow the night seemed to stretch out endlessly before them.

"Maggie?" His voice was soft and questioning.

"Yes?"

"Are you awake?"

"No. I always carry on conversations in my sleep." She went up on her elbow but she couldn't see him in the dark. "What is it?"

His sigh was full of some sort of ambiguous longing she couldn't identify. "I want you to tell me things," he said softly.

She smiled in the darkness. "A bedtime story?"

"No stories. I want facts." His voice changed. "Tell me things about you. I want to know everything. Tell me about your husband. I don't really know anything about your marriage."

She winced, turning away. "You don't want to hear about that."

"Okay, then how about your childhood?"

She sighed dramatically. "I was born on a dark and stormy night in a little log cabin in the woods...."

"Your real childhood," he said dryly.

She hesitated. She really didn't want to do this, but she supposed it had to be done sometime. Quickly, she went over her very conventional upbringing. "I was a Brownie. I took piano lessons. Attended City

College. Lived at home and commuted.'' She stirred restlessly. ''What else do you want to know?''

''Tell me about your parents.''

Now they were getting into a touchy area. She tried to keep her voice steady. ''My father was an accountant. My mother was a kindergarten teacher.'' Maybe he would let her leave it at that.

''Sounds like the ideal all-American family.''

She closed her eyes. Her childhood had hardly been ideal. Should she tell him?

''Did you meet your husband...what was his name?''

''Tom.''

''Did you meet Tom at City College?''

''Yes.''

He was silent for a moment, then he asked the inevitable question. ''How did he die?''

''It was a car accident. He was on a hunting trip with friends.''

''Maggie, I'm really so sorry.''

His voice was filled with true compassion and she felt like a fraud. She closed her eyes, fighting it, but the sense of cheating him wouldn't go away.

''Kane, I'm going to tell you the truth,'' she said, her voice trembling just a bit. ''The whole story. The unhappy things. And believe me, there were plenty of happy things. But I'm going to tell you about the worst and then I'm never going to talk about it again.''

He was silent for a moment, thinking over what she'd said. "Okay," he said at last.

She took a deep breath and launched into it. "My father was abusive…"

"What?" She could hear him sitting up.

"No, not physically," she reassured him quickly. "Verbally." She paused and he waited, but she could feel the tension of his emotional response to what little she'd already told him.

"This is so hard to talk about, because it's sort of one of those 'you had to be there' things. You say 'verbally abusive' and people think, 'So he yelled a lot, so what? All dads do that.'" She paused, trying to find a way to explain. "It wasn't always yelling. It was quieter, but more deadly. From the time I was a little girl, he tore me down in every way he could. He purposefully set up situations where I would fail, so that he could show me again how worthless I was."

Her voice faltered, and she coughed to clear it. "There's no way I can convey to you how destructive verbal abuse can be. But I lived it and I know. The old saying that words can never hurt you is a lie."

"How did your mother handle it?" he said when she paused.

"She didn't. She stayed away. She was always at a meeting or doing something in her classroom or visiting someone. And she left it to me to prepare his meals and take care of the house most of the time. So I pretty much got the brunt of his poison."

Kane didn't say anything, but his own anger was palpable. She could feel it simmering in the darkness.

"I married Tom partly to escape that awful house," she said calmly. "And my father. I know you're thinking, why didn't I just move out on my own? After all, I was twenty years old. I could have taken an apartment and a job and done fine by myself."

She hesitated, wishing she had better words to make this clear. "But you see...I don't know if you can understand this, but when you are being routinely verbally abused, you feel so small. No matter how much you tell yourself not to listen, the words flung at you sink in, and a part of you actually believes that you are worthless and dumb and ugly and....and...."

"Maggie..."

She could hear him moving and she said very quickly, "No, Kane. Please stay where you are, or I won't be able to finish telling you this."

He stayed and she went on.

"You feel as though you can't do anything for yourself. It's a very debilitating process once it gets going. You think you need to depend on someone else. And I depended on Tom." She shrugged, though no one could see it. "Maybe if I'd had counseling I could have stood on my own two feet. But I didn't. Instead, I married Tom."

"Didn't you love him?"

"Oh yes, of course. At first." This was the hardest part. "But...you know how they say a woman tends to marry a copy of her father if she comes from a dysfunctional family?''

She sighed. ''I'm going to sound like a whiner telling you this, but it is true. Tom turned out to be sort of a junior version of what my father was. He didn't drink too much and sit me down and harangue me with hour-long lectures on what a failure I was, like my father did, but he did try to control me in his own way. He had a knack for putting things so that they hurt me in the very place I was most vulnerable. And then he would do things like…well, he made it impossible for me to have friends, always objecting to my doing anything that didn't directly involve him. He would call up stores to make sure I really was where I'd said I was going. And if I objected to any of these things, he told me it was just that he loved me so much, he didn't want anything to happen to me.''

''I've come to realize it was his way of keeping me under control. He thought he loved me so much he wanted to keep me very close.'' There was so much more, but she didn't want to dredge it all up. It was over and done.

''Now, I'm only telling you this because you seem to have the idea that I may be pining away for Tom. Well, I'm not. I regret that he died. But I don't regret that I don't have to live with him any longer. I just wanted you to know that.''

''I'm so sorry, Maggie.''

''Oh, don't be. In some ways I blame myself for

it. I came to him in such a weak position, I was almost asking to be treated like that. But eventually I had something outside my home to cling to. I had my job.''

''Maggie, that's what I don't understand. I would never in a hundred years have guessed you had no self-esteem. At the office, you're a powerhouse.''

''Kane,'' she said, wondering if he could hear her affection for him, ''it's always been wonderful working for you. But it took a while, and gradual but consistent success, to make myself into that sort of person at work. And the more I pretended to have it all together, the more it became the reality. At the office, I was in control. But at home, I was a basket case. And then when I started working for you...'' She turned toward him with a smile in her voice. ''Working for you was what really brought me out, Kane. You helped me gain the confidence I needed.''

''I'm glad, Maggie.'' His voice hardened. ''But I wish I could blot out all the rest of it for you,'' he murmured angrily. ''I wish I could make it so that it had never happened.''

He finally understood why she had been so hesitant to marry again. He had his own reasons for not trusting marriage, but hers put his to shame. Here he'd been making a big deal over Crystal choosing money over love. So what? All he had to do was get rid of her. Maggie had lived in a nightmare.

''One more thing, Kane,'' she went on with quiet intensity, ''I want to make this very clear. I would never let myself live like that again. I've grown a lot since those days. I'm stronger. And I know I don't have to live that way. I won't.''

He didn't say anything. What could he do? Promise he would never treat her that way? What good were those sorts of promises? But he knew it wouldn't happen between them. He respected her too much. And he just couldn't imagine being that sort of man anyway. But how could he prove that to her at this point?

"Now you know all about me. But I know so little about you.''

"There's nothing to know,'' he told her. And he pretty much meant it. He was an open book, after all.

She hesitated. "I hope you don't mind, but Jill told me about Crystal.''

He winced. There was that. "Crystal? Who's Crystal?''

Maggie was sure he was just avoiding the issue, but just in case, she elaborated. "You know. Your first wife.''

"Never heard of her,'' was his immediate response.

Maggie sighed, then smiled in the dark. So Jill had been right. He wasn't going to talk about it. And here she'd gone on and on about her own past problems. Oh well, she'd told him now. She could put that away and not think about it again. And she did feel better for having told him. She yawned, sleepy all of a sudden.

"I guess it's finally time to go to sleep, isn't it?'' she said. "Goodnight, Kane. Sleep tight.''

"Good night, Maggie. Sweet dreams."

Kane sat in the dark for a long time, listening to her breathe. Even after he could tell she'd fallen asleep, he stayed where he was, listening. He'd wanted to comfort her so badly. He'd ached to take her in his arms and kiss away her pain—and maybe let her cry the unshed tears he had a feeling she still needed to release.

But he couldn't do that. If he did that, he knew very well he would be walking through a door that he'd vowed to keep barred—opening the very Pandora's box they had both sworn to keep tightly shut.

So he stayed where he was, filled with the totally male impulse to do something about what had happened to her, but frustrated. The men who had hurt her weren't available for any sort of revenge. And he couldn't take her in his arms without risking destroying their arrangement—an arrangement only two days old that was supposed to last for the rest of their lives.

The background she'd revealed haunted him all the next day.

He had declared their last honeymoon day to be dedicated to shopping. After all, she needed maternity clothes and a lot of new things for her move into his apartment. So they spent the morning going up one side of Michigan Avenue—the Magnificent Mile— had lunch in a cute little trendy spot and then worked their way back down the other side of the street, visiting every exclusive boutique along with each big department store.

Maggie resisted him spending too much money on her at first, but once she got into it, she seemed to develop a taste for shopping, and she began relishing it, admitting to him that she had never felt free to buy much for herself before.

He enjoyed watching her pleasure. It made him angry to think she'd gone through as much unhappiness as she had. But then, when you came right down to it, if it took that to make her into the wonderful woman she'd become.... No, he decided. It wasn't worth it. But it did give you something to think about.

She didn't mention any of her old problems during the day, and he hoped she'd forgotten all she'd told him. Everything they purchased was sent to his apartment and they returned to their hotel room in the evening pretty thoroughly exhausted. They took turns using the Jacuzzi, both thinking how much more fun it would have been to do it together, then shared a light meal in their room and went to bed early, falling asleep right away.

But just after midnight, Kane awoke with a start and listened. Did he hear her crying? No, but she was talking in her sleep. The few words he could understand didn't make any sense, but she sounded restless and unhappy, and he couldn't just ignore it. Slowly, he rose from the chair and went to her.

"Maggie," he said softly, taking hold of her shoulder and shaking it a bit. "Maggie, are you okay?"

"Oh," she said, raising her head. "What?"

"You were talking in your sleep."

"Oh." She roused herself. "Yes. I was dreaming." She shuddered. "Ugh. Not a nice dream."

He stood over her, torn. He could barely see her in the gloom. He wanted to stay with her, to comfort her. Her skin had felt like warm silk to his hand. He longed to hold her in his arms. But if he did, he knew very well what would happen. So he turned and went back to his chair, his insides tied in knots.

He thought she would go right back to sleep, but in another moment he heard her getting out of the bed and slipping into her robe.

"Kane, do you mind?" she asked him quietly. "Could I just open the drapes and let a little light in? I feel so claustrophobic all of a sudden."

"Sure," he said. "Go ahead."

She pulled them open, revealing the floor-to-ceiling window and the lights of the city sparkled before them, looking like a midnight wonderland of diamonds.

"Isn't it beautiful?" she said, standing at the window with her arms crossed over her chest.

"Yes," he answered, watching her. "Maggie, are you okay?"

"Oh sure." She half laughed, turning toward him. "I don't know what that was all about. I think maybe all those things we talked about last night brought up a lot of bad memories that I've pretty much suppressed lately. And once they were out in the open, my mind has to sort of shuffle them back down again. That's all.''

She smiled at him, then turned back to the window. He loved the way she looked in the moonlight. Her nightgown and robe formed a gauzy haze around the vague outlines of her body and her hair fell around her shoulders like a lacy shawl. But he could tell by the way she was carrying herself that her dream had affected her more than she was admitting. His heart went out to her. He had to do something about her pain.

''Maggie…'' He reached for her hand.

She let him take hold of it but resisted as he tugged her toward where he sat in the big overstuffed chair.

''Come here,'' he said, tugging harder. ''Come on. I just want to comfort you. You obviously need more than words.''.

Reluctantly, she let him pull her down to snuggle with him in the chair. He chucked her under the chin as though she were a little girl, just to prove his intentions were honorable. ''I just want to hear a smile in your voice again,'' he told her.

She looked into his eyes for a long moment, then sighed and let her head fall against his chest. ''It's your turn to tell *me* a story,'' she said, relaxing against him.

''Okay,'' he answered, breathing in the sweet scent of her body heat as it filled his head and forcing back the quick response his body wanted to make.

He thought for a moment, going back into his own

past, digging deep into his treasure trove of experiences, looking for something that might amuse her. Holding her in the circle of his arms, he began by telling her about the time he'd made a mistake and ended up taking two girls to the prom, dashing back and forth between the two of them, satisfying neither.

She smiled at that one, so he went on, telling her about his early boyhood attempts at the business world, selling home-made cookies to his friends. Imagine his surprise when he was accused by their parents of trying to poison the neighborhood when everyone coincidentally came down with chicken pox. This time she actually giggled.

"One more," she said, cuddling in more closely.

He forced himself to ignore how good she felt against him and thought hard, finally remembering the time he'd gone late to give a speech and in the rush, ended up giving a talk which included jokes about "cooking the books" to the wrong group—instead of the business gathering he was supposed to address, he was talking to a cooking club, all of whom looked very puzzled at his topic.

"It was pretty embarrassing," he told her. "But the ladies were very nice about it. They even invited me to stay for the quiche demonstration when the real chef finally arrived."

She laughed out loud. "And what about your lonely businessmen, sitting in some room waiting to hear about how to get away with accounting fraud?"

"It wasn't really fraud," he reassured her. "I was exaggerating."

She chuckled and he congratulated himself. Keep them laughing, he told himself. As long as she was laughing, maybe he could ignore the fact that this beautiful body—this beautiful nearly naked body—felt so good pressed against his. Now maybe she could get up and go back to her own bed and go to sleep with a lighter heart.

She sighed. She'd become so comfortable, she'd melted against him, as though her bones were made of wax. Tilting her head, she looked up into his eyes.

"Thank you," she said softly.

"You're welcome," he said back, but she was lifting her lips to give him a quick kiss, and suddenly his mouth was covering hers and the quick kiss turned out to be the spark that lit the flame that had been banked between them, a fire that had just been waiting for its chance to spread its heat. Her mouth was so hot, her skin so soft, her tongue so slippery. He'd been carefully avoiding touching her too suggestively, but now his hand slid right over her sweet round breast and his body came to life beneath her in a way she couldn't possibly ignore.

And she wanted him, too. Every sense told him so—the way her body arched beneath his touch, the way her breath quickened in his ear, the moan he heard deep in her throat.

He had to stop this.

"Maggie," he groaned, his breath ragged.

"Shhh," she whispered, placing a finger before his lips to quiet him. And then she began to drop tiny nipping kisses along the cord of his neck, and he knew he was lost.

They made love on the chair like two wild things, and then they lay together whispering and laughing, like teenagers who'd done something daring and found it dangerously delicious.

Then they switched to the bed and he pulled off her nightgown, feasting his eyes on how her breasts looked in the light that streamed in from the wide window, her beautiful nipples swollen and throbbing to his touch, and they made love again, this time so slowly, so sweetly, he thought he would die of pure delight. She fell asleep right afterwards, but he didn't.

He lay awake for a long, long time, looking at her. She was so beautiful and what they'd just shared had been so very good. He loved looking at her naked body, loved the swelling stomach where she carried his child, loved the long legs and graceful spine. His desire for her stirred again and he groaned, forcing it back. Making love to her had been better than anything he'd ever done. He couldn't deny he would do it again in a heartbeat.

But he couldn't let that happen. As he finally came to his senses, he was swearing at himself and anger swelled in his chest. He'd just violated his own rules. What was the matter with him? Now he'd risked ruining everything. This was supposed to stay platonic. The whole point was to avoid the fantasy world of love and love-making. It was supposed to be a business deal where they both knew what to expect from each other. Now who knew what she expected from him? He didn't even know what he expected from her. He might just have destroyed something very fine.

But maybe it wasn't too late. Maybe if he drew back...? He nodded slowly to himself. He had to draw back. Going forward like this was just too risky. What seemed so good at first could turn so rotten. He'd lived it and he wouldn't let something like that contaminate their relationship. She needed him to be strong, and he needed her to be wise. And that meant they had to go back to the way things had been before this happened. It had to be that way.

Chapter Nine

"Maggie, I hate to bug you on the day you get back from your honeymoon, but a lot of us are really upset about the rumors that the day-care center may not happen. Do you think that you could talk to Kane and see if you can find out what's going on?"

Maggie frowned. "Of course, Jen. I'll do it right away. I'll get back to you as soon as I know something."

Maggie replaced the receiver and groaned. How could she have forgotten all about this issue? She needed to find out the answer just as much as anyone else. But sitting at her desk, she hesitated. Kane was in his office and it would be a simple thing to walk in and ask him what the deal was. But something told her he wasn't going to be receptive to the question.

They'd been back at work since early that morning

and it was late afternoon now, but she and Kane had
barely had time to say two words to each other. There
had been all kinds of small disasters while they were
away and they were both busy trying to mop them all
up.

She'd woken up that morning in the hotel room and
the first thing she'd thought of was Kane's beautiful
body and the way they'd made love together the night
before. She'd never known love could be like that—
so warm, so gentle, and so exciting at the same time.
Kane was wonderful, and she was completely in love
with him.

What had happened to her hesitation, her apprehension, her fears? The slate hadn't been wiped clean.
They were still hanging around underneath her current happiness, ready to jump back out if they were
needed. But she was hopeful again. Things were looking good.

"I'm just a fool for love," she admitted to the
morning, stretching her arms over her head and rev-
eling in her memories.

Kane was in the shower. She could hear the water
running. She waited a few minutes, then remembered
that she had her own bathroom. Laughing at herself,
she'd gone ahead and taken her shower, too. By the
time she was up and dressed, it was getting late and
they'd had to hurry to make it to the office in time
for a conference call Kane had scheduled the week
before.

In all the rush, Kane had seemed distracted. She'd

hoped they would be on a new level of affectionate intimacy because of what had happened, but she'd seen no evidence of that as yet.

Still, she could certainly understand that it might take a while for them to settle into their marriage. There would be ups and downs—that was only natural. She could wait. The happy glow from the night they'd spent together would sustain her.

And yet, she had to admit that something was keeping her from dashing right in to talk to Kane about the day-care center. She wasn't sure why, but she was having a hard time doing it, finding lots of little jobs that needed to be done first. When she stopped to think about it, she realized she was avoiding the issue, and that wasn't good.

"Enough dawdling," she told herself at last, pushing up and out of her chair and heading for his office.

He'd had the door closed because he was taking calls and she rapped sharply on it before pushing it open and walking in. There he was, bent over some papers, his brow furrowed as though things weren't going well at all.

"Kane," she said, walking in to lean on his desk. "I'm getting questions from people about the day-care center...."

"What about it?" he interjected sharply, his attention still on the letter he was going over.

She blinked, surprised at his tone. "They are saying that we might not be getting it."

His face didn't show annoyance, but there was no

warmth there either. "Look, I'll handle that. Just give me some time. All hell is breaking loose here."

She knew there were problems. There had been a small fire in a storage room and Coldair, a major client, was angry about some billing they disputed and was threatening to change accounting firms.

"Sorry," she said quickly. "I know you're busy. But if I could just give people some reassurance that you're working on it...?"

"Maggie, I said to leave the day-care center to me."

She was taken aback. He'd never spoken to her so shortly before. It was obvious that whatever was going wrong with the day-care center, he was stressed out about it—along with everything else.

"Yes sir," she said, giving him a military salute and turning on her heel to go back to her desk.

"Maggie, wait a minute," he said, and she turned back with a smile, sure that he was going to apologize.

But she was disappointed again. He merely frowned as he shuffled papers and said, distractedly, "You know that Coldair is giving us a lot of trouble. It looks like I'm going to have to go deal with it personally. So I'm going to have to go out of town for a few days."

Her heart fell, but she understood. Some things just couldn't be helped. This was business.

He frowned again, shaking his head and finally looking up to meet her gaze. "I'm sorry to do this just when you're moving into the penthouse. I called Mark. He'll help you move your things.'' Rising, he took her shoulders in his hands and planted a kiss on her forehead. ''I've got that suitcase that I always keep packed for emergencies, so I won't have to go home first. I'm taking the next flight out for Pittsburgh. Sorry about this, Maggie.''

She knew this was part of being involved in negotiations and business affairs and it didn't really surprise her. But…was it her imagination or was there a new coolness to his manner? And if so, why?

She ate her dinner alone in the penthouse, wandering from room to room, wishing it didn't feel so empty. Kane had obviously had a decorator take care of the furnishings and everything looked like layouts from an upscale magazine, but she would have liked to have seen some personal touches somewhere in all the twelve rooms. Just from the looks of things, she doubted whether Kane had ever spent much time there except to sleep and clean up in the morning. How was she going to turn this place into a home?

She chose her own bedroom—not having had any input from Kane and not wanting to presume so much as to sleep in his bed. There were four of them. She supposed she could try a different one for every night Kane was gone.

Why didn't that sound like fun? It should have. But she had a feeling nothing was going to be much fun until Kane came back.

Mark came by the next evening and took her over

to her old apartment to gather some things together and prepare for the movers to bring over her boxes. Mark was in quite a chatty mood and seemed tickled that his big brother had married Maggie.

"You've married a great guy, you know," he just happened to mention as they drove from one apartment building to the other.

"I know." She smiled, thinking of Kane. "I have worked for him for two years, remember."

"Sure." He nodded, but he was still looking at her as though he thought she didn't really appreciate what she was getting here. "I've known him for longer. And I'm telling you, he's a great guy." His brows came together as he thought that over.

"He's a good businessman. Runs a really quality company. And that's partly because of his superior management skills and instincts." He smiled as they came to a stop at a light. "He is a little impractical sometimes," he added, looking over at her. "A little soft-hearted where he ought to be more hard-headed."

"In what way?" Maggie asked curiously. She knew he was sensitive in ways she'd never imagined before their honeymoon, but she wasn't sure what Mark was driving at.

"Well, take this child-care center thing he's been pushing for his company." The light changed and Mark started up the car again. "There's no way that's going to fly. He's already getting mired down in problems. They're going to have to drop it."

Her heart sank. "You don't mean that! Why?"

He shrugged. "Can't do it. The lawyer has said it's too much liability to carry. There is going to be all kinds of trouble with it." He pulled into Kane's parking structure. "There's almost a guarantee that someone will sue. A kid will get hurt on the kiddy slide or someone will offer peanut butter to a kid who's allergic to peanuts or someone will claim the day care worker is showing preferential treatment to all the children except hers. There's always someone who thinks they might have a chance at striking it big. Like winning the lottery. And they ruin it for everyone else."

"That's such a shame," Maggie said, shaking her head. "How did we get into this position where one person's greed can take something good away from everyone else?"

"It's a real problem." He pulled into the parking space and turned off the engine. "But what can Kane do? The liability is just too overwhelming. He can't risk losing the entire business over a day-care center."

Maggie swallowed hard, deeply shaken. "I suppose not," she said sadly, but she wished she could think of some solution.

The situation was so depressing. She knew that many of the women at Kane Haley were depending on the day-care center, planning their lives around it. Jen had called her again that very day asking what she knew about it. She wouldn't tell her friends what

Mark had said just yet, she decided. Better to wait and talk to Kane first.

In the meantime, she could hardly wait for Kane to get home. She missed him so much! He called every evening, mostly to hear about what had happened in the office that day, and he seemed rushed and tired, and on the third night, he had bad news. He was going to have to go down to Florida to put out another rebellion among clients, and since he was due to appear at a conference in Fort Lauderdale the next week anyway, he might as well just go straight to it. That meant it would be over a week before she would see him again.

"I'm a lucky guy, you know," he told her lightly. "I know you're holding down the fort, so I can afford to take this much time away from the office. If it weren't for you, I'd be agonizing over this."

The compliments were nice, but not enough to make up for not having him home again. Swallowing her disappointment, she held back her comments and tried to remain cheerful. She knew he didn't like doing this any more than she liked having him do it. She wanted him home so that they could get back to the business of building their marriage.

Every night she was falling asleep with memories of their one beautiful night together playing over and over in her head like a movie. What she was looking forward to most was the sequel.

Kane was back. The elevator bell rang and she looked up and there he was, striding toward the office, looking like the handsome man she'd married. Maggie threw down her pen and jumped up to greet him.

"Welcome home, stranger," she said, beaming at him.

"Maggie." He stopped before her and for just a moment, she was sure she saw affection in the depths of his dark eyes, a warmth that could have curled her toes. But almost immediately it was gone and his eyes glazed over, flat as the panes of a tinted window. She lifted her face for his kiss and he landed it on her cheek instead of her lips, then turned and headed for his office.

Maggie stood where she was, stunned. There was no use trying to deny it any longer. All the old excuses she'd been using wouldn't hold. He was purposely freezing her out.

At first, she was numb. It took a few hours for her to come to terms with what was going on, and then she decided to wait until they were home to approach him about it. This wasn't something she wanted to talk over in front of others.

But it wasn't something she could ignore, either. When she'd ignored things in the past, the results had been very bad. She couldn't let things drift. If he had changed his mind, if he regretted having married her—a thought that cut like a knife into her soul— she wanted to know right away.

She waited until after dinner to talk to him. She'd prepared a big pot of spaghetti with meat sauce and he ate two helpings. That, along with the fact that he seemed perfectly willing to talk about his trip and ask her in a friendly manner about what she'd been up to, helped make her wonder if she were seeing things clearly. He seemed fine.

Except that he never touched her. And he never looked at her as though he wanted to.

Another big hint—when she showed him which bedroom she'd chosen for herself, he approved her choice and didn't say, "Aren't you going to sleep with me?" How she would have loved to have heard those words. But he didn't utter them, and she knew that pretty much confirmed her fears. He didn't want her in his bed. That hurt in a deep, burning way that bewildered her.

After dinner they sat on his modern leather couch in front of a roaring fire and listened to light jazz and talked a little more about what was going on at the office. And finally, she steeled herself and brought up what was most on her mind.

"Kane," she said, trying to hold his gaze with her own. "Are you sorry we did this?"

He looked startled for just a second. "Did what?" he asked her.

"Got married."

Something flashed deep in his gaze, but she couldn't identify what it was.

"No, of course not," he said quickly, but his gaze shifted away from hers. "Why do you ask that?"

"Because you seem to want to keep me at arm's

length. I'd almost say you were avoiding me at times.''

"That's ridiculous. You know how I feel about you, Maggie.''

"No, Kane. I don't. I wish you'd tell me.''

He was quiet for a long moment, staring into the fire. What did she want from him? He was trying very hard to keep the equilibrium they had both agreed they needed for the stability they had to have, and now he was feeling a bit morose and unappreciated.

Didn't she understand how hard it was to stay away from her? They'd both agreed from the beginning that it would be for the best if they kept their relationship platonic. That way they wouldn't run the risk having to deal with the complications, the highs and the lows.

But he sure did miss those highs! That night in the hotel…he ached whenever he thought of it. Being near her was sweet temptation mixed with exquisite torture. He was hoping the intensity would dim with time, and they could go on without entanglements. But she wanted to know how he felt about her right now.

Well, how did he feel? Did he love her? Love wasn't something he thought about a lot. He supposed he did love her in a way. But he'd once loved his first wife, Crystal, too. What did love matter? Love didn't stop bad things from happening.

For a few days, he'd seen a vision of a possible future that seemed too good to be true. He didn't dare count on it. Where people were concerned, you

couldn't count on anything. He knew he had to protect himself and hold on to the things he knew he
could depend on—work and his money. That was it.
Nothing more.

Finally he turned and looked her in the eye. "Maggie, we made a bargain, remember? This is purely a
business arrangement."

Something in his tone shocked her. "But... I
thought...after that night in the hotel..."

His gaze didn't soften. "We made one mistake.
That doesn't negate the entire agreement. I think we'll
both be happier if we stick to the plan. Don't you?"

Happier? Was he kidding?

She sat in silence for a long time, then excused
herself and went to her lonely bedroom. Slipping under the covers, she turned off the light, but she knew
very well she wasn't going to sleep for hours. His
words were echoing in her head. This was just a business arrangement. No loving allowed.

Well, darn it, he was right. That had been their
bargain and she supposed she ought to keep her end
of it. She'd been just as determined to insist upon it
at the time as he had.

But that had been before they'd made love. And
once she'd given her heart and soul to him, didn't
that make things a little bit different?

Obviously not. He'd said it himself, that women
always take that sort of thing much more seriously
than men do. She should have taken his words to
heart. Maybe she *had* been silly and female.

"So sue me!" she said aloud, looking up at the dark ceiling with a scowl.

And yet, she knew that on a level of logic and clear thinking, he was right. Well, okay. She would be stronger. She would survive. And she would stop projecting things onto him that he didn't have any time for. She would stop asking for things he couldn't give. If that was the way it had to be, she could take it.

But what would that mean for her baby? Putting two loving hands over her stomach, she felt movement, and she had to smile despite her pain. Her baby was the point of this entire situation. Right now she was so confused it was very hard to think through all the ramifications. If she just continued working her way through, day by day, maybe it would all work out for the best in the end. Sure, things would be okay.

But if everything was so hopeful, why were tears spilling down her cheeks? She wiped them away angrily. She wasn't going to cry, darn it all! She was going to concentrate on her baby. That was all that was really important, after all.

Jill knew something was wrong right away. She came by the office to take Maggie to lunch, and, after downing a very large cheeseburger and two plates of fries, she ordered cherry pie à la mode and demanded Maggie tell her what the problem was.

"And don't give me that 'nothing' routine," she

said crisply, digging into her dessert. "Your eyes are full of misery. You can't hide it any more than a snake can hide the bulge from that fat rabbit he just swallowed."

"It's stupid, really," Maggie told her hesitantly. "I don't think…"

Jill nodded and cut right to the chase. "You're in love with Kane, aren't you?"

Maggie bit her lip, playing with the silverware. "Yes," she said softly.

Jill snorted and took another bite of pie. "So much for 'modern platonic marriages.'"

"Oh, but he doesn't love me."

"Really." Her tone crackled with skepticism.

"No, he doesn't. He wants us to keep this as a business arrangement. He's been very clear on that."

Jill sighed and pushed her plate away. "Nothing's clear to Kane right now. Kane's head has been full of fuzz ever since he found out he was going to have a baby." She pursed her lips. "Has he told you about his father yet?"

Maggie shook her head. "No. He doesn't like to talk about his past."

"Then I'll have to fill you in on that, too." Jill set her elbows on the table. "Here it is in a nutshell. He adored his father. There was some special attachment that happened because his father drank too much and even as a little boy, he felt protective of the old guy. Then his father died in a traffic accident—he was drunk, of course—and Kane felt it as an abandonment. He's never really gotten over it completely. Their mother told this to Mark when they were young—explaining why Kane was being moody and had hurt Mark with something he said. Kane's still hung up on losing his dad. End of story.''

Maggie blinked at her. ''Well that's very sad, but I don't see—''

''You don't see how that gives him a special feeling for this kid you're carrying?''

''Sure, but—''

''You don't see why that makes him afraid to commit to you for fear he'll lose you, too?''

Maggie thought for a moment and shook her head. ''Not really.''

''Think about it. It will come to you.'' She waved one hand in Maggie's direction as she signaled the waiter for the check with the other. ''In the meantime, don't give up on him. He's worth the effort.''

Maggie was sure he was, if only she knew what effort she really ought to make to create the climate they could come together in. He'd married her because he wanted ties to his child. She was just a means to an end. How could it be otherwise?

The answer finally surfaced for her. He didn't love her the way she loved him. And maybe he never would. It took a few days for her to come to terms with what was happening, but once she did, a feeling of dread began to grow in her chest. Could she stay with him if this was the way it was going to be?

The problem was, they were so busy, she hardly

had time to think about her own doubts and fears. And despite everything, their relationship was genuinely friendly. Except for the first day they'd been back, he hadn't been short or angry with her at all, and her vague fears that he might resort to the sort of verbal attacks she'd known with her other male relationships began to fade away. He wasn't going to be that way.

In fact, many women would have been perfectly happy with what they had together. What she was missing was that extra level of warmth she'd assumed would come after their one glorious night in the hotel.

Had that night really happened? Sometimes she wondered if maybe she had dreamed it.

The day-care center issue was still up in the air and she didn't want to broach it with Kane at this point. She'd looked through some of the files while he was still away, and sure enough, Mark was right. All the lawyers had recommended against going forward with the day-care center. They'd been quite strong in their opinions. They'd written that establishing the center would just be asking for trouble Kane didn't need. There were too many fires to put out in their business situation today, and with the tightening economy, the competitive climate, and the amount of legal sharks always circling in a search for vulnerabilities, it would be crazy to go ahead with something so risky.

Well, of course, his business came first. Without it, none of them would have jobs, much less child care.

So she wasn't prepared to argue with him about it. But she wished, deep in her heart, that something could be done.

Jen and Sharon cornered her in the break room one day and demanded to know what was going on.

"Listen, Maggie, we know you're very busy, but we really need an answer on this. If you can't find out yourself, we're going to have to go to Kane directly."

Maggie sighed. "You can do that, of course. But I have to tell you, from what I've heard so far, things don't look good." Briefly, she explained about the lawyers' opinions.

"This is just so unfair," Sharon said in frustration. "Can't you say something to Kane about this? Can't you convince him?"

How could she tell them that she was afraid she no longer had even as much pull with him as she had when she was only his administrative assistant? Neither Sharon nor Jen seemed to want to see things from Kane's point of view and Maggie felt as though she had to defend him. Still, she understood how they felt. She was just as upset as they were.

So she was caught completely by surprise when one day in late March she found two men in work clothes wandering the premises, looking lost.

"Can I help you, gentlemen?" she asked.

"Yes," said the older man. "We're from Branart Construction. We're looking for the day-care center."

"The day-care center?"

"Yes, I think we've got the wrong floor." He held out a requisition form to show her what was marked there.

"You do have the wrong floor. But tell me, why are you looking for the day-care center?"

"We're preparing for the new round of renovations you've ordered. We need to take some measurements and start drawing up final plans."

The younger man chimed in, "We've got a tight deadline since the official opening will be in June. We'd really like to get started right away."

"There must be some mistake." She took the form again and studied it. The date was just two days old. "Funny," she murmured, but she quickly showed them to the elevator and sent them to the correct floor.

Something very strange was going on. Could it be...?

Turning, she hurried back to her office and rushed right through to Kane's. He was on the telephone, but she didn't wait.

"What's happening with the day-care center?" she demanded.

He hesitated, then told the party on the other end of the conversation he would get back to him, and hung up the phone, watching her the whole time.

"What is going on?" she said again.

He leaned back in his chair and gave her a slow grin like she hadn't seen in weeks. "What's put this bee in your bonnet?" he asked her, one eyebrow raised.

"Will you tell me?" she cried, frustrated. "I thought there were problems. Insurmountable problems."

"Sure there are problems. There are always problems."

"But…"

He rose from his chair, his eyes sparkling with amusement at her agitation. "Did you really think I was going to let them take the day-care center away from us?" he asked as he came toward her. "Did you think I would let all my employees down?"

She stared at him. "But your business…you could lose it. At least, that's what they were saying…."

"If anyone tries to close us down, we'll fight it," he said simply, smiling down at her. "Listen, I didn't get where I am by running from challenges. When something is important to me, I'll take my chances."

He was going to keep the day-care center! He was going to fight for it. He was a hero! He'd never looked more handsome than he did to her at that very moment.

"Oh Kane!" She threw her arms around his neck.

"Hey," he said, teasing her. "Watch the suit."

But his arms came around her and he looked down at her soft mouth and the two of them came together as though something stronger than they could fight was pulling them. His mouth on hers was hot as a summer sun, intoxicating as a shot of brandy. She opened to him as though she'd been waiting for him all her life, and right now, she just about felt as though she had been. She needed him so badly, needed his kiss, needed his strength. His hard body was paradise and she melted against him like a supplicant at the gates.

Her fingers sank into his thick hair, pulling him even harder against her, and his hands slid down and took possession of her bottom, tucking her into the hard hunger of his hips. Her senses swam in a river of sweet desire and she moaned low in her throat, devouring his mouth with her own. If he'd have her, she would take him right there, wrap her lonely body around him and surrender to his claim.

She was his. Didn't he know that?

Voices in the hall finally penetrated the sensual fog they were enveloped in and they pulled reluctantly apart. In another moment, people filled the office, laughing and talking and presenting some sort of problem to Kane. Maggie didn't stick around to find out what it was. She slipped out and went to her desk, holding close the knowledge that Kane wanted her. At least there was that.

Chapter Ten

And still it took Maggie a couple of weeks to come to her senses. Thinking back on it later, she blamed it on being pregnant.

"All those crazy hormones were messing up my thinking," she would tell herself. But once her thinking did clear, she knew exactly what she had to do.

She knew she couldn't let events overtake her again. She was beginning to think there must be something in her that brought this controlling impulse out in men. But she knew she couldn't let herself be treated as a cipher. She had never been able to stand up to her father, or to her first husband. But she was a different woman now. And she would stand up for herself if it killed her.

That evening she joined Kane as he read the newspaper on the terrace. It was a warm evening and a breeze was blowing. They sat in silence watching the sun's last reflections in the windows of the surrounding high-rise buildings.

Maggie closed her eyes and tried to gather strength. She knew what she was risking by confronting him. He might just shrug his shoulders and tell her to take a hike. And then it would all be over.

But she had to do this. She couldn't live in fear. She'd done that too often in her life.

"Kane," she said at last, turning toward him. "I want to break our contract."

He looked at her over the newspaper he was reading. "What are you talking about?"

"I've already broken the terms of our agreement. The entire issue is null and void for all practical purposes. Things have changed between us."

His face darkened. "Nothing's changed."

"Yes it has." She lifted her chin. "We agreed to a loveless marriage, and I've broken my word. I've...I've fallen in love with you."

The words had seemed impossible to say, and she'd been worried that she wouldn't be able to get them out. But now that she had, she felt a flood of relief. It was out in the open. She'd done it.

But he wasn't saying anything. He was staring at her as though she were a ghost. If only he would kiss her. If only he would smile and tell her that he loved her, too. But as the seconds ticked by, she realized that wasn't going to happen.

"So you see," she told him bravely, her voice wavering only slightly. "We're going to have to start over."

"Maggie we've talked about this," he said at last, his face expressionless. "We both agreed it would be best if we kept emotions out of it."

"Easy to say. Hard to do."

"Yes." He stared into her eyes for a moment, then frowned and shook his head. He knew what she wanted from him but he couldn't do it. Even if he wanted to, he just couldn't. Still, he wanted to do something to show her how he felt about her. Maybe he couldn't do what she was asking for, but there were other ways to manifest his affection.

"Look, I know what." He put the newspaper down. "I meant to do this before, but I got so tied up with business. I'm going to open a couple of credit cards in your name—"

Her head went back and she gasped. "What? You think I want your money?" She could hardly believe he could be such a bad judge of her character. "I'm not Crystal, Kane. You can't buy me off."

He looked at her in surprise, then realized he should have known better. What was he thinking? "Maggie, wait. I didn't mean—"

"Do you think this is just a way to manipulate more money out of you?" she demanded, bewildered and hurt. "Do you really think I just want to pressure you to give me things?" She swallowed hard and her hands formed fists at her sides.

"Well, guess what," she said quietly. "Funny, but

you're right. That's exactly what I'm doing.'' Her jaw set, she glared at him again. ''But Kane, what I want out of you is not your damn bank book. What I want is your heart.''

She didn't wait this time. She could already see his answer in his eyes.

''I love you, Kane, and if you don't love me back, it's over. I can't live like this. I'll go as soon as the baby is born. I'll stay nearby so that you can be a father to our baby. But I won't live under your roof if you don't love me.''

She rose and turned to go. At the sliding glass door, she paused, closing her eyes and praying he would call her back. But he didn't say anything, and she went on to her bedroom.

Kane watched her go, his heart like lead in his chest. He felt paralyzed. He couldn't speak. A strange detachment held him, as though he were watching a movie he'd seen before. A part of him wanted to reach out for her, to tell her how he felt about her. But he couldn't do it. He sat where he was, as cold and useless as a stone.

On the whole, things were moving along apace. She and Kane were on friendly footing, as though nothing had ever happened. Maggie's friends at work were planning a baby shower for her. She'd called and made arrangements to begin natural childbirth classes in a few days. Though it was hard to believe eight weeks had passed since their wedding. She was seven and a half months pregnant. It wouldn't be long now.

The baby was kicking all the time, making her laugh, making her gasp. Sometimes she felt as though he already had a personality, and she found herself crooning little sayings to him when no one was listening. She and Kane had chosen a bedroom for the baby and decorated it with stuffed animals and a mural of a happy-go-lucky bunch of circus animals. On the surface, to the casual onlooker, everything would seem to be going very well.

It had been a weird day for April. Spring was breaking out all over, and yet she'd gone through the motions of her work feeling as though she had a little black cloud tagging along above her head. Something just felt out of whack. Deep inside she had some sort of apprehension brewing and she didn't know why.

"Here, have a pickle," CeCe offered as she came into the break room that afternoon where many of her friends were gathered for a late snack.

Maggie looked at it and blanched. "No thanks."

"No? I thought pregnant women always loved pickles."

"Not this pregnant woman." She felt slightly sick in a way she hadn't felt since the first few months of her pregnancy. With a shudder, she left the break room and took a short walk around the floor, trying to find some way to start feeling better.

And then the queasy feeling began to change into a crampy sensation, and a tiny, growing sliver of fear began to flit around the edges of her mind. Somehow it wasn't that much of a surprise when she went into the bathroom and saw the blood.

Sharon had come in behind her and was fixing her hair at the mirror. "Have you heard about plans for the grand opening of the day-care center?" she was asking. "I hear there will be food and balloons and clowns for the kids. It will be so much fun."

"Sharon," Maggie said, coming out and leaning against the sink, feeling faint. "Please get Kane. I think something's wrong."

Sharon gasped. "Ohmigod. Oh, Maggie, are you okay? I'll get him. Wait here!"

"Please hurry," Maggie said urgently, sinking to sit on the lounge couch and doubling over with pain.

And then everything became very confused. There were sirens and Kane's voice, but she wasn't sure where she was or what was happening.

The next time her mind became clear, she knew right away she was in a hospital bed. There were tubes connected here and there, to her hand and to a band around her waist and monitors were making strange noises. The first thing she did was reach down to press her free hand to her stomach. Yes, her baby was still there. Relief flooded her and tears welled in her eyes.

And suddenly Kane was bending over her. He looked strained and worried. She smiled up at him, wanting to tell him not to worry, but how could she when she had no idea what was going on? Something felt very wrong and her smile slipped away.

"Maggie, they are doing everything they can to try to keep the baby in where he belongs as long as possible. But don't worry about him. His vital signs are fine."

She nodded and closed her eyes and went back to sleep again. It seemed safer to stay in dreamland for a while.

Kane sank back into the chair drawn right up next to her bed, rubbing his hand against his unshaven chin. This had been his home for the last twenty-four hours, and he wasn't leaving until everything was all right. And it had to be all right. It had to be.

Maggie woke up again. She'd been sleeping so much lately she wasn't sure what day it was. She heard people talking. They were saying something about danger to the baby, but she kept drifting off again before she could pin it down. Then she heard Kane talking to Jill and she opened her eyes and smiled at them both.

"Hi," she said. "How's the baby doing?"

"Fine," Kane told her, grabbing her hand and holding it tightly. "How are you?"

She was going to fall asleep again. She could feel it coming. But she wanted to tell him something before she slipped away. She'd been dreaming about it and she wanted to make sure he knew.

"Kane," she said, clinging to his hand. "I know you'll never love me, but I want you to know, no matter what happens, you will always have your baby. I will never try to take him away from you in any way. I promise you that."

He leaned close and kissed her and her eyes closed. Straightening, he looked at his sister-in-law. "Where the hell did she get the idea that I would never love her?" he demanded, his dark eyes tortured.

Jill shrugged and gave him a fake smile. "I don't know. Maybe when you started treating her like the cleaning lady instead of your wife."

He scowled. "That's ridiculous."

Jill sighed. "Kane, wake up. You're a very smart man but you must be blind. Why can't you see that the very things you're doing to protect yourself from being hurt are guaranteeing that that very hurt will be inevitable?"

"I don't know what you're talking about."

"Yes, you do." Reaching up, she kissed his cheek. "And I have faith that you're going to do something about it. Right away." She turned to go. "See you tomorrow. Give me a call if anything happens."

He nodded glumly, sitting back down in the chair and staring at Maggie. Jill was annoying as hell, but she was so often right about things. If he was honest with himself he'd have to admit he'd been so busy protecting himself against the chance that Maggie might leave him that he'd set up the circumstances to push her into doing exactly that. What kind of an idiot was he, anyway?

Reaching out, he smoothed a strand of hair back

off Maggie's perfect forehead. And his heart swelled with love.

Maggie woke up and looked around the room. A nurse was bustling in with a tray.

"Awake? Wonderful. Just in time for your lunch."

Maggie frowned, wondering how she was going to eat anything, then noticed that the nurse hadn't meant it literally. She was busy attaching a new glucose drip to the IV that was stuck in Maggie's hand.

"Yummy," she murmured, trying to smile.

"That's what we like, patients with a sense of humor," the nurse told her with a laugh. Then she stopped beside the bed. "I have to tell you, honey, the whole floor is talking about that husband of yours. Talk about devotion. He lives in that chair." She gestured toward it with her head. "He hardly ever takes his eyes off you."

As though on cue, Kane appeared in the doorway.

"And here he is now," the nurse said, giving Maggie a wink and moving on.

"Maggie." He came to her and bent, and she lifted her lips for his kiss. "Oh Maggie, I wish you didn't have to go through all this."

"It will all be worth it if the baby comes through okay," she said.

He hesitated. "Maggie, are you awake enough to understand if I explain what they're planning to do?"

She nodded, suddenly anxious.

"They are going to have to take the baby in the

morning. Your system just won't calm down and get back to normal.''

She fretted. "It's too soon."

He nodded. "I know. But it can't be helped. There's too much danger in waiting any longer." He drew her hand to his lips and kissed her fingers, his dark eyes holding hers. "Maggie, we'll be okay. We're in this together."

"But if he dies...."

His fingers tightened around hers. "Maggie, we'll still have each other. We can have another baby." He kissed her fingers again and went on, his voice husky with emotion. "But there will never be another you. I need you to make it. You promise me."

She felt as though she were in a dream. She tried to focus but she was so sleepy. "Tomorrow?" she said.

"Yes. In the morning."

"We haven't decided on a name," she said groggily, fighting to stay awake a few more minutes.

"What would you like to name him?"

She thought for a moment, then remembered something she'd been planning before all this happened. "What was your father's name?"

"My father's name?" He looked surprised. "Benjamin."

She smiled. "Benjamin it is." And then she was asleep.

He stared down at her. What on earth had made her say that? She couldn't have said anything more perfect. Benjamin. His father's name. Somehow that closed a circle for him and his heart was lighter than it had been for days.

God, but she was good. How could he not love her?

He was so nervous the next morning, he was jumpy as a cat. Maggie was being prepped for surgery and he had to stay out of her room while they were going through the preparations. He stood outside the door, scowling, until the nurse told him he could go back in.

"They say I'm going back to sleep again," she told him sleepily. "All I do is sleep in this place."

"This time we'll have a baby when you wake up," he told her, taking her hand in his.

She nodded, looking pleased.

He looked down into her beloved face and the truth came pouring out. "Maggie," he said, his voice choked. "Maggie, I love you."

"Do you mean that?" She squinted at him. "You're not just saying that because the doctor told you to say it so I'd be in a better frame of mind for my surgery?"

He groaned. "Maggie, no one could get me to say I love you if I didn't mean it." He gathered her into his arms and held her tenderly. "I love you. And for some stupid reason I haven't been able to tell you or show you." She felt so small, so frail in his embrace. Could she survive this? If he lost her....

Suddenly he could say the things he'd wanted to

say to her. Suddenly it was as though a floodgate had been released.

"Maggie, I love you more than life itself," he told her urgently. "If anything were to happen to you, I think I'd die."

"You won't die." She smiled. "But I might just die of happiness."

"You're going to have to leave the room, Mr. Haley." The nurse was very stern. "It's time."

Reluctantly, he released Maggie's hand and began to back out of the room.

"Take good care of her," he said fiercely.

As Maggie sank into unconsciousness, she had a smile on her face, because Kane's last words hadn't sounded much like a request—but more like a threat.

Jill stayed with Kane while they waited. He paced just like a traditional father, and she surreptitiously took pictures of him doing it to show Maggie later. And both of them spent time in silent prayer, because the outcome was by no means certain,

By the time the doctor came out in his green scrubs, Mark had joined them and they all rushed to greet the doctor anxiously. He grinned. "This is the part I love," he quipped. "I feel like a rock star."

"How is she?" Kane demanded.

"She's doing fine. And you've got a beautiful baby boy. You can see him in about an hour. He'll have to spend some time in the neonatal unit, but his Apgar score isn't bad for his age. He should be fine."

All the blood seemed to drain from Kane's face and Mark and Jill grabbed him, afraid he'd fall to the floor.

"I'm okay," he told them ruefully. "I'm just so damn relieved...."

When Maggie slowly regained consciousness, she found Kane at her bedside and she came wide awake in a hurry.

"Kane?"

She was in his arms before she'd finished saying his name. "Everything is fine, darling," he said, kissing her eyebrows, her temple, her ears. "Benjamin is the most beautiful baby you've ever seen and he's going to be perfectly normal. I swear to you."

She sighed happily. "When can I see him?"

"As soon as they think you can make it. The nurse will get a wheelchair and I'll take you over."

She nodded. "Kane?" she asked, twisting so that she could see his face.

"Yes?"

"Do you still love me?" She smiled at him. "Or was that a dream I had?"

He laughed low in his throat. "I still love you, Maggie. And when I get you home and you're well enough, I'm going to love you all over."

She giggled. "You promise?"

"You want me to put it in writing?"

"No!" she grimaced. "No more business contracts. I'll take your word for it."

She looked into her husband's face and searched

his eyes, wanting reassurance that this was for real and that it wouldn't slip through her fingers this time. What she saw told her not to worry. Kane had gone to another level and learned to trust a bit more than before.

Reaching out, she laid a hand along the side of his face. She loved him so very much. And now she had hope that they were going to have a real marriage and make a real family. No more business arrangements!

"I'm so lucky," she told him. "As I look back now, I was having a baby for all the wrong reasons. And you came into the picture and made them all right."

He kissed her, and she closed her eyes and let herself float in his love.

It was later in the afternoon when Maggie was finally allowed to ride over to the neonatal unit to see her baby. He was in an incubator, but it hadn't been necessary to hook him up to a ventilator. Still, he was being watched very closely and would probably not be able to go home right away.

Maggie was allowed to hold him and she cooed over him, beaming with joy. "He's so gorgeous!" she cried. "Look at his tiny little fingernails. Oh Kane, I think he looks just like you."

"Lucky devil," he teased. "Just as long as he has his mother's personality, we'll do okay."

She cuddled the baby close, her heart filled with more joy than she'd ever known before. "Kane, how many more babies shall we have?" she asked.

"Babies? Plural?"

"Sure. You don't think we're going to stop at one, do you?"

He hadn't ever thought about it before. He frowned skeptically. "A house full of kids?"

She nodded happily. "Tons of them, tumbling all over the place. The boys copying everything you do and the girls twisting you around their tiny little fingers." She sighed blissfully. "You're going to love them."

And suddenly he realized she was right. He was going to love them. Just as he loved her and little Ben. He felt very strange and then he realized what it was. For the first time in his life, he was a completely happy man.

* * * * *

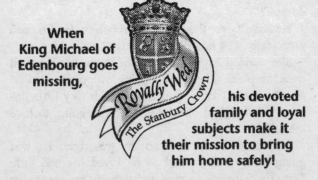

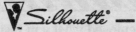

Silhouette Romance introduces tales of
enchanted love and things beyond explanation
in the new series

Soulmates

Couples destined for each other are brought
together by the powerful magic of love....

A precious gift brings
A HUSBAND IN HER EYES
by Karen Rose Smith (on sale March 2002)

Dreams come true in
CASSIE'S COWBOY
by Diane Pershing (on sale April 2002)

A legacy of love arrives
BECAUSE OF THE RING
by Stella Bagwell (on sale May 2002)

*Available at
your favorite retail outlet.*

Silhouette ®
Where love comes alive™

Visit Silhouette at www.eHarlequin.com
SRSOUL